BOG

BY DOONVORCANNON

Photo by Егор Камелев on Unsplash.

Cover by Doonvorcannon.

Table of Contents

For Sixela, greater than Erato

Chapter 1

Some Day

Does the spider love? My spider claimed to. Bog wanted me to sit in my room and do nothing. Is that love?

Of course. To do nothing is better than to lust.

I stuck my finger into my ear and Bog crawled onto my fingertip. He barely took up half the surface area of my fingernail. I held my finger up and stared at him. He blinked. His eyes gleamed like polished coal.

"This has nothing to do with lust," I muttered.

The bus was mostly empty save for an elderly couple in the front. Even still, I hunched lower in my back corner.

I do not want you to sit in your room and do nothing. I meant that it would be better than to do what you are about to do.

I scoffed and turned to glare out the window. The light of the early morning was blood soaked. The town was cast in a gory hue that unsettled me. I trembled and looked back at my finger. Bog blinked. I stuck my finger back into my ear.

Could a spider love? Could humans? Could anyone? I felt like I loved her. Her. But what about him? With Bog back inside my head, I couldn't help but wonder at his purpose. Maybe he loved others, but he sure didn't love me. It seemed like I always went against his requirements for love. He seemed to be against love. He was certainly against my love of her. He called it fantasy, nothing but lust. I paused and tilted my head, waiting for him to interject. He remained silent. Perhaps I was on to something. Perhaps the spider couldn't love.

The bus squeaked to a slow stop and I hastily scurried out. My mind was only on her now. She should be around soon. The old rowhouses stared rottenly at me. I turned to stare into the park. I smiled at the sophisticated live oaks with their Spanish moss waterfalling down like luxurious hair. I felt at home here, not on those streets. The park was an oasis. It somehow floated above the poverty and crime that surrounded it. My heart quickened and I swallowed. Bog grumbled from inside my ear canal. Or brain. I could never tell. He was too small.

I knew that she'd be here soon. I went and climbed the same tree that I always did. She couldn't see me up here, but I could see her. I liked to imagine that she knew I was there and kept coming back for me. Sometimes the feeling felt realer than my own reality. That sometimes was more of an often than not.

No good chimpanzee. Fling your dung.

I ignored his insults and clung to the tree limb.

She's false.

His whispers went silent as her body glided into my vision. Sixela the Great. A Greek goddess that for some reason had never been named in mythology, probably because she was never a myth. The reason she visited my town and this park every morning tantalized me. It was for me. Or was it for her, by being for me? Was my for me, really a for nobody? If she didn't know I was here, then what was she doing? I'd been happy enough to gaze at her these past few weeks.

Sixela's skin and dress glittered translucent. Her dress was bone white and shined with a silver aura. She was brighter today. Her countenance like a clear opal, I leaned off my branch to soak in her radiance. I imagined her scent was of wine and olives. Her skin was golden-bronze, yet ghostly in its near transparency.

She's false.

Her black hair violently torrented behind her, caught in the wind like a stallion's mane. Or the wind was caught by her hair. She commanded all. My chest hurt so much that I winced. A thunder clap of blue shot at me. Her irises burned brighter than the flames of Hades. I shuddered, a wave of orgasmic electricity singeing my palms. My grip loosened and I collapsed onto the ground. She stepped up to me. She looked at the tree and not at my sunken form.

My skin's yellow-pink hue paled sallower. I tried not to picture myself. I closed my eyes. I could see my form, my pathetic thin body jagged like the guillotine prepared to end all hope—my hope severed—she stepped over me. My hair was crumpled in an awful part, revealing my mountain forehead.

"Hello Bog," she said.

Hello Sixela.

She and Bog spoke inside my head, their voices pinging about as alien thoughts.

She was looking down, not at me or through me, but at the inside of my skull. Her eyes focused where Bog no doubt was resting in my brain. Her lips crinkled, and her mouth remained closed. I breathed in, swallowing her sunny ocean-mist scent greedily.

Am I false?

Her voice was an operatic whisper, impossibly loud and divine as if a chorus of angels spoke as one in a seductive murmur. My eyes were wet. She did not see me.

You lie.

Bog's voice took on a different tone. Usually his voice whispered like the summer breeze that wasn't quite there. Now he roared like the winds of a hurricane.

"We've fallen from our pinnacle. Yet you watch us as if we are not true when you are the one lying," she said. "I do not tempt when you do not do."

We? We? Was she referring to me? I shuddered but couldn't bring myself to move. She still wasn't looking at me but at my skull. I thought I saw her mouth twitch as if teasing a smile at my excitement. Was the we referring to Bog? I was pretty sure I was the one who'd fallen, sprawled lamely on the ground as I was.

"Sixela?" I mumbled, my face redder than blood.

She smiled at me, her teeth cloud white and round, each one glinting like an individual pearl. She turned and fled, laughing gaily as she skipped off. Her laughter sang from outside my head as she left me.

Wake up you fool. She is false.

I didn't bother acknowledging him. I stumbled to my feet and brushed my chest.

Who do you think helped you up?

"Not you," I said.

Her beauty had knocked me down but her grace had brought me back. All I could think about was her skin, so smooth and soft. If marble was of flesh, it would still fall short. Sixela. Sixela. How could I think of anyone or anything else when someone and something so beautiful existed? Grinning, I drifted out of the park and wandered. I didn't want to return to my apartment. Not yet. Not with Sixela so alive and out here. Unfortunately, it was the tail end of early morning and people were beginning to shuffle about.

I tried not to look at them. Their cars whirred mechanically. Indifferent faces seemed to turn away yet stare at me all the same. Could I not walk alongside the road in peace? Are sidewalks not meant to be walked on? My smile ached and it crumbled into a frown. Another car passed with a heavyset woman eyeing me as if my frail frame were an affront to her decadence—an insult to her health. I straightened my mouth and allowed myself to go blank, my body as mechanical as the buzzing cars.

I'd never forget the day I'd first met Sixela. As though in a dream, I had been sitting in the park, writing poems on a bench. I had been writing a foolish piece, romanticizing my only girlfriend, if I could ever even call her that. A girl that I had dated when I'd been very young, and broken up with that same year. It was so pathetic that I never bothered trying to rationalize it. I'd stumbled upon her social media through a mutual friend and had been swept up in a flood of limerence that grew and grew until it became a whirlpool without bottom. Simply put, she was beautiful and I'd stared at her beauty, my heart pouring into my mind.

But there was more. She was of a religion I had once dreamed of joining, though I had been too afraid to ever take the leap. My fear had always kept me from others. And my fear had stirred something inside me—a myth of beauty and longing that had me lost in illusion and fantasy. So, there on that bench I imagined that we we're destined to be together.

My lips twitched at the memory and a smile started to reform. I recalled the words of that poem I wrote that day directly.

Irises aglow with divinity,
your eyes burn femininity

so radiant I'm blind.

The sun aligned,

I can look at nobody without you on my mind.

Eclipsed, I drift out in orbit and ellipse.

The forgotten satellite,

I send out empty signals without light—

so I write and write and write.

My words lost in the dark of night.

Sixela the Great is too great for me.

The last line had materialized from a mythological desire. I wanted divinity. The name blossomed. Was that the girl I had known? Well, when I had looked up from my notebook, Sixela was standing there far away. At the time I'd only seen the back of her, and what a sight it was. Each morning I returned to that spot; the more hidden I was, the more of her I saw. Until now.

"Good morning," a suit-person said.

I stuttered and hung my head, walking brisker. I hadn't been looking at the person so why bother me? The person furrowed into their suit until there was nothing but suit left. No head or arms or legs, just suit. I stalked my way into downtown. The sidewalks were even more uncomfortable now. Thin and concrete, they left me little room to avoid pedestrians. I was forced to slither around the occasional passerby. Tired of dodging, I ducked into a bookstore. Nobody was at the register. I walked to the corner and crumbled into a plush black chair.

Sinking, I sighed, finally at ease and hidden from any nosy eyes or needling sounds. And Bog was quiet. Quiet. Beautiful. Warmth. I faded deeper into the black of the chair. A slight rustling sound pulled me back. On the shelf above my head sat a tiny green lizard with its face buried in a book. The book was placed in front of the lizard, and the rustling sound I heard was the lizard's tongue turning the page.

"Excuse me," I inquired.

"Oh my!" the lizard shrieked as it skittered between two books on the shelf behind it. "Did I disturb you?" Its head peeked out and its voice was a chirping whimper.

I smiled. The lizard had disturbed me, but the fear on its face was enough to melt my annoyance. Its head seemed to vibrate it twitched so nervously, and the little lizard's eyes darted everywhere but at me as if looking for someone to blame. It remained mostly hidden in the books, and it looked absolutely adorable. I giggled.

The lizard seemed to take offense at this and slithered out into the open. It straightened itself, stretching its small frame as if to intimidate me. The lizard gazed directly at me and ceased moving to the point of looking like a little toy someone had left behind.

"I am Detherwheel, and I do not take so kindly to your lack of respect. If you keep this up, I might have to kill you."

I giggled louder. The lizards odd chirp sounded unnatural, as if it weren't used to speaking or making any noise at all. Its threats didn't exactly make me tremble like its tiny head had been doing before.

Detherwheel is a he, not an it.

"Of course," I muttered. "I knew it was too good to be true."

Bog crawled out of my ear and jumped onto the shelf, standing right next to Detherwheel. Bog had better be careful, that lizard could eat him right up and that'd be that. He was the tiniest spider I'd ever seen. Even this minuscule reptile was a giant to him.

"You've fallen low. This worm is not worth keeping in your web," Detherwheel said.

I frowned and shivered. The chirping was more of a bark now. I swallowed and tried to remain as calm as one could be in a situation such as this. I might be someone with a spider living in my head, but even I had my limits.

You are only low when you think worms aren't worth it.

"This one seems to be a bit lacking," Detherwheel said.

Detherwheel, why are you here? What is it you want?

"Am I not allowed to read here?"

I propped myself up on the chair and leaned forward till the two of them were right in front of my face. Bog's four eyes were squinted and he glared knowingly at the lizard.

With a huff, Detherwheel turned his entire body to face me. "Would you like to go on an epic quest with me as your guide?"

Still sighing, he half bowed his head. He then waited there expectantly with his head tilted like a judgmental cat. I couldn't discern if it was in jest or not.

"Are we going to go someplace magical," I said in a faux childlike voice. "Is it down a rabbit hole? Or maybe hidden in some dusty wardrobe? To the mirror!" I stopped and rolled my eyes. How could this speck kill me? I was annoyed with myself for letting such an unassuming creature mess with me.

Bog hadn't ceased glaring at the lizard, apparently uninterested in my little display. Detherwheel remained in the same position, not betraying any emotion other than an apparent air of boredom. We all stared at each other without awkwardness, just a shared indifference.

Who put you up to this?

Bog's tone made it sound like he already knew the answer to his question. I leaned closer.

"You know who."

She is false.

"Sixela!" I shouted. The lizard cowered, bending its body into a crescent while Bog glowered at the both of us. "Where do we go? We must go at once! She mustn't be kept waiting!" My words tore through the quiet of the bookstore.

I stuck my nose at Detherwheel and waited. My body tensed and my skin reddened. Sixela. The goddess wanted me to go on a quest? What could she want? Why? The answers didn't matter. What mattered was that she knew who I was, and that she deemed me important enough for this… whatever this was.

"You want her," Detherwheel said, still folded in the same position.

I frowned and opened my mouth to speak. Bog jumped inside, landing right on my tongue without so much as a whisper. Not wanting to crush the tiny spider, I froze with my mouth gaping. He crawled down my throat and I didn't move until the itchy feeling of his hairy legs dissipated. Coughing softly, I scratched at my cheek. Never before had Bog done such a thing. His home was solely kept in my brain, with my ear canals as his doors.

"Excuse me," I said.

"She's at your home. You must go home."

"That's my epic quest?" Raising an eyebrow, I couldn't help but wonder if Detherwheel was pulling my toe.

"And as your guide, I've decided that I'm done guiding. Go home."

Detherwheel slithered in between the books and was gone. I didn't bother looking for him; I was already on my way out the door. As soon as I went outside, I instantly regretted it. The streets were eerily empty. No cars, no people. I gulped and looked above. The sky was no longer sky. The heavens were mountains. Literal peaks and valleys filled the expanse above, with the ragged mountaintops pointing down like fangs in a closing maw. There was sky in between, and that was all that buffered the ground I stood on and the ground in the sky. My stomach heaved as the terrible thought that I was the one upside down came to me. I ran back inside.

The bookstore was empty. To call it a bookstore would be foolish at the moment. Now, it was simply an empty room lacking any furnishings. Just bare floors and walls. I turned and went back out the door. Sadly, the vacant streets and mountain sky remained as before. Gulping, I started walking back towards the park. I found myself wishing Bog would offer some sort of consolation here; even a good reprimanding would be welcome at this point. Everything was silent. No birds, no wind. The only sound audible to my ears was the increasingly obnoxious banging of my heart. I tried not to look up and stared at my feet as I moved. The park was where I needed to go. My home was too far to walk back to. Maybe I'd find Sixela there. Any sign of life would be nice. Even that strange suit-person. Even that stupid lizard.

"Why are you heading back to the park? I said you must go home!" Detherwheel shouted, his voice muffled in my shirt's sleeve.

I yelped and grabbed the reptile by his tail, yanking him through the neck hole of my shirt and tossing him to the ground. He bounced off his back and spent several seconds blinking, before finally looking up at me to sneer.

"Where am I? What did you do?" I asked.

If not for the unbearable silence, I would have stomped on him. But truthfully, his intrusion was a welcome one. This was not somewhere I wanted to be left alone.

"You're on your quest," he said, his tail curling in front of his face as he inspected it for damage.

"I thought you were done guiding."

"I am. I'm just here for the ride. The book I was reading was getting to be quite dull."

I didn't believe a word Detherwheel was saying. He had his own agenda in this, no doubt. His attitude seemed unfit for whatever it was that Sixela had sent him to do.

"Is a tiny little lizard really the best guide for an 'epic quest'?" Smiling, I was glad that my humor had returned. The jagged sky seemed less imposing with this ridiculous reptile curled in front of me. He was still examining his tail as if ogling pearls.

"May I have your permission to climb aboard?" he asked, dropping his tail behind him and creeping up to my foot.

"Just stay outside my clothes and on my shoulder where I can keep an eye on you."

"But it's so cold without the sun!" he cried, hesitantly lurching up my leg till he perched himself like a sentry right near my head. His tail draggled down and tickled the base of my neck.

"There's still a sun, it's just in the middle sky." I coughed to hide the tremor in my voice.

The sun here was cold and pallid. This wasn't the city I knew. The air was as empty as the streets. The humidity had dissipated and the air was arid and stank of spoiling meat. It wasn't cold, and it wasn't warm. Temperature seemed too natural for this place. It simply felt like… nothing. Like a stale nothing. My sudden noticing of the nothingness seemed to intensify it. My body ached and the landscape in front of me shimmered so quickly I wasn't entirely sure if it had.

"That's no sun. It's a lie," Detherwheel whispered. He made no effort to hide his whimpering.

I stared at the sun with my eyes wide open, standing as still as I could. The longer I looked the more certain I was that it wasn't a sun but a giant ball of... something. The sun was no sun as no light came from it. The light here, wherever here was, seemed to just exist in a pale and inert way—owing its origin to nothing or nobody in particular. A black speck that seemed to be growing glided across the surface of the false sun. Not wanting to be caught staring, I hung my head and pressed forward. I figured if I looked at my feet and at the apparently normal sidewalk as I made my way, I'd be impervious to the constant changes and absurdities whirring around me.

"What is this place?" I said, expectantly waiting for Detherwheel to reply. He hummed and curled himself snugly on my shoulder like a kitten.

I'd made the mistake of taking my eyes off the ground, and suddenly there was no surface beneath me. By the time I looked downwards, I was falling. No, that wasn't it. I was flying but only upside down. Or falling right-side up. In any case, I screamed as the mountain peaks came ever closer to my dangling feet.

"Just close your eyes!" Detherwheel shrieked, exuberance and mirth lifting his voice into a screech sharper than the scratching of a chubby child's fork on an emptied dinner plate.

I closed them and soft ground suddenly met my feet as if I'd been standing the whole time. I opened my eyes, expecting the worst, but to my delight, I was standing in a valley imbued with shades of violet and blue flowers that waved at me in the breeze. The breeze! There was a breeze now! The air was sweet and cottony as if it could be held in my arms and tasted.

And I noticed that the mountains this close up weren't mountains at all but mere foothills. There were six of them in total, and they surrounded the valley in an even, circular pattern. At the summit of each hill was a well; each one uniquely designed. The wells covered the entire tops of their respective hills.

"I guess we won't have to worry about water," I remarked.

"You'll have to worry about much more than that," a voice from above thundered.

I gulped. The sun in the sky was gone; all that remained was an empty expanse of gray. Well, mostly empty. A giant skull-like planet was suspended in the emptiness. Or maybe it was just a skull that was as large as a planet. Either way, it was a giant human skull and it had just spoken to me.

Chapter 2

Nothing

"Are you a planet or a skull?" I said.

The planet-skull didn't answer, it just kept smiling. It was
the kind of creepy smile that all skulls seemed to wear; a
permanent and mirthful grimace. I stared in awe as its jawbones
slid downward and its mouth opened wide.

"Inside my well. You must go to the moon-skull," a voice
whispered. The words cut through the air and cracked in my ears
like a whip, yet somehow remained impossibly faint.

The voice had come from the top of the nearest foothill, but
I could see nothing there but a well. I shrugged, almost forgetting
that Detherwheel was curled up there. The lizard harrumphed as he
was forced to cling tight as I scrambled to the well.

The well in question was a garish looking thing. Its bricks
were an ashy purple that simultaneously appeared offensively

bright and dejectedly lifeless. It had a black roof with absent tiles that revealed rotting wood beneath it. I peered down over the edge to see if there was anything in there. Just blackness.

"Inside! Inside!" Detherwheel said.

He jumped off my shoulder and into the black of the well and quickly disappeared, my outstretched arms reaching for his tail in vain. The air seemed to lose its lightness and cheer now that I was alone with only that infernal skull looming in the sky like a slowly approaching meteor. Was it my paranoia, or was the skull getting closer? Where was Sixela in all of this? She was the reason I was on this quest. I didn't care all too much for the rest.

Rubbing my head, I adjusted my hair as if I expected Sixela at the bottom of the well. But who knew, anything could happen the way today was going. I ran my hand over my bangs again, trying to make them as appealing as possible—which wasn't much on the best of days—and I jumped.

Or hovered in black space. I didn't know. The light from the top of the well was gone as if it had never existed. The fall was taking too long. A terrifying scenario played itself out in my mind.

What if I'd been falling here for an eternity, constantly living with the expectation of change without the slightest clue or reason how to bring about that change? Was my today really a forever? I couldn't even muster up the energy to despair. Instead, I let my mind consider Sixela's beauty. Her eyes shining like beacons, always drawing me in. There was an unrelenting deepness there that was dangerous. Her waist-length hair as dark as the raven's feather; it was darker than the abyss I was currently falling in, yet it shimmered unlike the deadness surrounding me. My heart fluttered as I considered the perfection of her body, and I gulped. With a shake of my head and a long stretch of my arms, I tried to bring myself into the present, however far off that present currently was.

I found it odd that I hadn't seen Detherwheel anywhere yet. I wondered how much further down he was and if he was still falling too. My wondering about the lizard must have hastened my fall, because the next moment I landed with a surprisingly painless thud into a pile of something hard and crunchy. I tried to roll out of the pile unsuccessfully. I wanted to die. It wasn't a pile I had landed in but an ocean. An ocean of skulls. There was no source of light above us, but the skulls carried a white effulgence of their own. For endless miles and miles, all that I could see were skulls pooled together like a macabre ball pit.

"Took you long enough," Detherwheel growled as he scurried out from a skull's eyehole and onto my shoulder. "The skulls don't even go up to your waist, quit your crying."

I wiped a tear from my eye and took a deep breath, focusing on the splendor of Sixela and all that was promised if I finished this infernal quest. Detherwheel was right; I could stand just fine, but that wasn't exactly helpful. There was nothing around us but these skulls.

I stared at the skulls nearest to me, quite impressed by their pure whiteness. It was as if they had been recently polished and sheened. One skull in particular caught my eye. It wasn't white but red. I reached for it and screamed. The skull was warm and wet, and a quick glance at my hand proved my fears true. My hand was imprinted with what could only be blood.

"I'm Death," the blood covered skull said, sounding like a sultry young woman with enough husk to make a cornstalk blush. The blood on Death's head bubbled and moved in ripples, cascading onto the skulls surrounding it. I stumbled backwards.

"I wish you wouldn't be so scared. Give me a second, and I'll be ready for you."

"Would you give her a second!" Detherwheel yelled into my ear.

Not really seeing a better option, I stopped retreating and watched. Her blood-soaked skull arose, pushing through the pile of white bones. A snakelike spine that was attached to her skull writhed into the air and floated. As she hovered like a ghost, blood poured from her in torrents, pooling close to where I stood. A whimsical tune whistled from the sea of skulls like wind blowing through their hollow mouths.

Death she grows, so red. So red.

Death she crows, you're dead. You're dead.

Her blood belongs to all that lived.

Her flowers feast on what you'll give.

Detherwheel hummed along to the shrill chanting of the skulls. It sounded like a deranged lullaby. After singing the lyrics three times, the song finally ended and the blood stopped flowing. Organs, sinew, muscles, and skin formed before my eyes until a beautiful woman hovered there naked. Her head was still a red skull but her body was perfection. I was intoxicated and couldn't, wouldn't look away. Much to my chagrin, she laughed at my lust, and flowers burst through her skin, blooming into rich, white roses. Only her red skull remained untouched by the flowers. Her eyes were no longer empty holes; they had transformed into two black eyeballs.

"I'm Death," she said again, floating closer to where I stood and reaching her flower drenched arm down towards mine.

I chuckled to myself. "How could you be Death when you're covered with life?"

"How can you be living when you're constantly dying?" she retorted, pulling back her arm. "Why have you come here?" she asked.

Not wanting to trade riddles with her or to incur her wrath, I put my hand to my heart and bowed my head. "I'm on a quest," I said without looking up.

"A quest for what?"

"A quest to go home."

"If I might add, he's on a quest of lust!" Detherwheel said, giggling gleefully.

"Of love!" I said with a blush.

"Or limerence," Detherwheel said, laughing again. "Limerence! The boy needs to rinse those limbs of his, he's making a mess of himself! Do you have any blood to spare, Death?"

"Who is this quest for?" Death asked, drifting higher and closer to me until she floated directly above.

"For Sixela," I said. It was like speaking with a cloud of flowers. That was all I could see at this point.

"She's not real!" Death shrieked, cackling so severely that flower petals rained down on me. "Enough about you, let's talk about me, and me is hungry. Please forfeit your life if you wish to continue on this make-believe quest of yours." Death descended until her red skull was eye-level with me.

"How can I continue on my quest if I'm dead?" I asked. Detherwheel giggled.

"Don't get lost in the details. Your life is mine… or better yet, your life is death." Her jaws creaked and her mouth grossly spread into a triumphant grin.

"Wait just a second!" a baritone, dust-soaked voice cried out. It came out muffled, apparently buried beneath the skulls. A black ten-gallon hat poked up through some skulls nearby.

"You!" Death yelled as she turned to face the hat.

The hat now had a man sprouting beneath it. He looked like some second-rate western character, garbed in a black cowboy outfit with two black revolvers as big as his head that he gleefully gripped in his hands. He had them both pointed at Death.

"I reckon you're not ready to die yet, partner," he drawled.

I rolled my eyes at the affectation he was putting on in an attempt to pull off this whole spaghetti western act. I glanced at Detherwheel and saw that the lizard was as unimpressed as myself. He was shaking his head and muttering "phony" under his breath.

"Why don't you turn around, fool," Death said.

Behind the wannabe cowboy were three heads that had risen from where Death had bled.

"That's why I have two guns," he said, pointing a revolver at the skulls while keeping the other trained on Death's head.

Floating skulls in teams of three arose to the left and right of the cowboy, and he grunted as if welcoming the added challenge. He shifted his black booted feet so that his black spurs were each facing the other direction. He looked like a lame chicken the way he was standing there. A little gun barrel popped out of the spur of each boot. I didn't see how that could work or would be very accurate, but Death seemed taken aback. Her eager grin turned into a frightening frown so drastic that I was shocked her jaw didn't detach itself from the rest of her skull.

"You're lucky my hat gun isn't working. Unfortunately, my pants gun is currently having some difficulties." He winked at Death and she... blushed? I might have imagined it, but that red was looking a bit rosier.

"Life, why do you have to interrupt this nobody's body's dying?" Death said as the skulls dropped lifeless to the ground.

"Living and dying, aren't we a pair!" he laughed, sporting a toothless grin. I was surprised he didn't spit tobacco out with a mouth like that. He holstered his guns and swaggered over to Death.

"Can't you ever let me finish?" she said.

"Nope. You can't finish what is already finished." He embraced death and the two of them collapsed into one skull, split vertically with one half black and the other red.

"We're still stuck here," I muttered, not impressed by the ridiculous display we'd just witnessed.

"A nice skull," Detherwheel tittered. I frowned at him. "Harmony and such," he said self-consciously.

"This doesn't help me finish this godforsaken quest. And I still have no idea where we are."

"The infinity of skulls surrounding you doesn't ring a bell?" he said.

A crashing sound of clanging bells bellowed out from beneath us. We rapidly sank and as the skulls closed over my head, the chiming bells clanged together like the thundering hooves of a stampede.

A herd of bell-cows thundered below. They were cows with bells for heads. Detherwheel and I hovered in the air, suspended above them all. From what I could tell, we were in a damp, dark cave.

"You were saying?" I said.

"We're in the moon-skull, you fool! Now pick a bell-cow to ride further along."

"Why are they literally bell-cows?"

"Why are you literally insane?"

I coughed. He had a point. "What about that cow?" I said, pointing at a big brown one with a silver bell head.

Most of the other cows had bronze or gold heads with white fur bodies, though I did spot a few pink ones. This one was the only brown one. Milk was great and strawberry milk could be good, but chocolate milk was my favorite. A loud ringing filled the air, a poor substitute for mooing as far as I was concerned.

"Descend! Descend!" Detherwheel cheered, bouncing on my shoulder till we lowered to the ground right next to the brown cow.

Before I could speak, a pink cow with purple spots jumped in front of me. "I'm Essthet! Do not make the erroneous choice of choosing that cow. Its color is all wrong. Do I not shine? Do I not sparkle?" Essthet twirled, her golden bell head tingling delightfully like delicate windchimes. "Choose to ride me, for is it not wise to choose what is most delightful? Choose delight! Think of the aesthetics! How envious others will be when they hear us coming! Imagine how much pleasure we'll have fulfilling your quest! Is that not your purpose? To fulfill it? Why not fulfill it with the utmost pleasure?"

"Excuse me," I said, stepping around Essthet.

The brown cow was fat and quite ugly. Its silver bell was rusting and when it moved, I didn't hear ringing, just a slight clicking like a shoulder popping out of place. But the smell of the bell-cow! Delicious, delectable chocolate! Much richer than the overwhelming strawberry-plum aroma that exuded from Essthet.

"So nice! So nice! Fine, fine, roll your dice! That old coot hasn't had a rider, ever!" Essthet harrumphed and trotted away.

I was glad to be rid of the cow. She had no manners. Besides, I wasn't being nice. I just liked chocolate milk.

"Am I the mooiest cow? Why, I'm the mooiest cow of all! The belliest of bell-cows that ever mooed!" The brown cow's voice was hoarse. A stark contrast to the sing-song chimes of Essthet.

"Can we ride you?" I said. The cow rang sharp and brittle and I covered my ears until the ringing subsided. "It's for a quest."

"Hop on!"

"Your name?" I said, bowing and feeling foolish for doing so.

"Moocha. Now hop on!"

Despite myself, I smiled and climbed on like a child, and Moocha galloped off. The other bell-cows parted in two perfect lines and mooed enthusiastically. Or rang. Regardless, I wished I could cover my ears but I was gripping Moocha too tight. The bell-cow moved with shocking speed and it was all I could do not to fall off. I heard Essthet's chimes rise above the rest; a harsh insulting sound as if she wanted me to fall off. Then, darkness struck my face and I was enveloped in complete silence and nothingness. Moocha, Detherwheel, and everything else was consumed in the black.

"Moocha?" I whispered. I could no longer hear the cow ringing. Even my voice was gone. My question was just a thought, I think.

All feeling had been swallowed into the surrounding abyss. My body was gone. I couldn't even recognize my thoughts as my own. My self had no relation, and I felt a dissipation tug and pull at my—at whatever I was. My being, or what remained of it, was being stretched into a nothing. What was I? Could losing all senses destroy my sense of self? Without sense or body, I was as empty as the darkness. I gave in. I gave in to despair and meaninglessness. And I floated. Float. Or not float. Verbs died. I just was. Or what remained of I just was.

Why was I? Why? The why was everything; without a why there was nothing. Was there no why? Could I make something in this darkness? Darkness is absence. A nothing. A nothing. Could I make something of nothing? Become a god? Why not smile at my dissipation? Sixela. Sixela. Her name was toxic on my tongue, yet sweeter than sin. A hope. A hope only leads to despair. Could I be myself without a future? Was a future a nothing? I laughed. Laughed hard. My thoughts guffawed, burning in the black of eternal night. Then, a light burst, and I returned as if I never was, the nothingness forgotten.

Chapter 3

Dust

Detherwheel was back on my shoulder. *My* shoulder. I was a me again. That was nice. Something nice. I smiled. Detherwheel stared. I frowned. Neither something or nothing was nice, and was nice necessarily better? My frown deepened and Detherwheel chortled.

"At last! The grand mall of the skull-moon," he said.

Now that I was myself again, I could see what spread out gloriously before me. A lascivious display of decadence glittered temptingly. If the mall were a woman, I'd propose and then worship her. Its ceiling was miles above and made of rolling waves of striped gold and silver that spiraled and whirled about in a shimmering froth like the ocean's surf. And on the ground, there were kiosks… kiosks abound! The kiosks dotted the vast floorspace like magnificent islands. All the kiosks had roofs that were different shades of violet, each glowing with its own gem-like brilliance. There were no walls that I could see, only kiosks spreading out endlessly. The floor however, was disappointing. It was a rather plain, ridiculously polished, beige linoleum.

"So, what's the plan? Better yet… what's the point?" I said with a dry chuckle.

"Open your eyes, you blind mouse," Detherwheel said, hopping and pointing towards the kiosks.

I staggered backwards. Empty suits and dresses moved around as if invisible people wore them. They appeared to be shopping and browsing; every kiosk had at least one suit-patron.

"What does this mean?" I said.

A blue suit with red pinstripes at the closest kiosk turned towards me, its red tie waggling about like a venomous tongue. It stiffly limped over to me.

"Why did the stiffest suit here have to choose to talk to us? The humanity!" Detherwheel cried, shielding his face with his tail.

"What do you want?" I said.

"Step inside," it rustled, the suit creasing with each syllable. Its tie stretched out to touch me but I stepped away.

"No," I said.

"Do it," Detherwheel said.

"No."

The suit smelled like plastic. Its tie stretched out further, hanging in the air like a rattlesnake poised to strike. Detherwheel climbed on my head and wacked me with his tail.

"No!" I screamed with a tired ferocity. This game had run its course and I wasn't playing it any longer. "No!" I screamed louder.

The suit's tie fluttered back and whimpered. The suit folded and collapsed onto the ground in a ragged heap. It suddenly stank of rot. The infinitude of suits and dresses all turned towards me; their rumbling rustle coursing through the air. I covered my ears at first, but plugged my nose next as the smell of decay struck my nostrils. I vomited onto the collapsed suit in front of me. My eyes burned as I stared. The suits and dresses all fell to the ground silently.

"Don't move," Detherwheel whispered from atop my head.

I decided to heed his advice for once and stood as I was, keeping my fingers stuffed in my nostrils. Dark red shapes blurred in front of me. I moved my eyes to follow one of the shapes and quickly regretted it. The shapes were monsters covered in bubbling boils that spouted out blood. There must have been thousands of them, crawling around and skittering about like lion-sized cockroaches as they sniffed the fallen clothing. Each one of the beasts was a grotesque blob of puss with four scaly claws. Their mouths were filled to the brim with yellow-brown fangs, and they had snake-like tongues that licked greedily at the clothes.

Two of the foul beasts scuttled towards the suit in front of me, and they sniffed at the vomit drenched clothes. My heart quickened and tears streamed out of my eyes at the overwhelming stench of these spoiled meat lizards. An eruption of blood from one of the lizards shot out and hit me in the face, and I yelped. A horde of the monsters ran towards me but suddenly stopped at the clothing.

I somehow hadn't moved during my involuntary shriek. The disgusting blood was dripping down my face, repulsively close to my lips. I then noticed that the lizards didn't have eyes. Why weren't they attacking me? My shriek and smell should have given me away.

"I'm done with this," I muttered. Holding my breath, I wiped the blood from my face and rolled my shoulders. "I'm done!" I yelled.

"What have you done!" Detherwheel cried.

The monsters pounced on me. Covering me with their saliva and blood, they tore apart my body. Like the black nothingness from before, I drifted inwards and away from the painful filth ravaging my flesh. I drifted deeper, deeper still. Even in my own darkness, I could still see the monsters crawling along the walls of my mind. They filled my darkness, always nearing but not quite crossing over into my drifting. The smell was worsening.

I gritted my teeth and snarled back at the foul beasts. Could they not even give me respite in my dying ego? I screamed and spat. I seethed. I swung my fists at the cold darkness, the monsters loping out of my reach yet never ceasing their pursuit as I continued drifting into the abyss. My heart struck my chest angrily, and I swung my fists in the air. I screamed. I burned. I hated. I hated it all. I hated everything. Why was I here? Why were any of us here? The nonsense quest! The nonsensical lies of supposed reality!

I struck myself in the chest. Angrily realizing that I couldn't reach the monsters scuttling about, I turned my fury onto myself. Hammering at my chest, I howled. Spittle flew and I kept striking myself, my darkness darkening into nothing. A true nothing. My rage rose higher and I awoke.

"I told you not to move," Detherwheel said.

I sat up and looked around. I was sprawled out on a cushy leather couch in a comfy looking office. Detherwheel was staring at me suspiciously from his perch on top of a large black desk. The desk was made of expensive looking wood and it towered over me. It was engraved with Greek tragedy masks that showed every kind of emotion. Every inch of the wood was covered with the eerie etched faces.

A large black leather chair behind the desk was turned away from me. I shuddered. Someone was clearly in it. Forgetting the horror of the monsters from before, I swallowed and decided to speak.

"H-hello?" I said.

The chair turned and I was faced with perhaps the most surprising sight yet. It was myself... or a copy of myself. The disheveled, thin brown hair and long narrow face grinned down at me. His eyes were a dark marble green but they appeared far off, as if there were no hint of life behind them.

"At least you look normal," I said with a forced chuckle.

I put my hand to my chest which was exceedingly sore as if I'd had a heart attack or something. Then I recalled how I'd been beating it in that insufferable darkness. I shuddered and wrapped my arms around myself.

"I'm monstrous vermin morphed into man," he said, wagging his finger at me like an impatient school teacher.

"You look like me." I sat up on the couch and snarled.

The rage from the darkness was gnawing at my bones. I gritted my teeth. I was doing everything in my power to stay seated and to not stand up and strangle this imposter.

"You look like me too! Though I used to be much more beetle-like. This form has its drawbacks. I do miss scavenging for my beloved trash! The smell was so sumptuous!" He clapped and shivered, an unnatural smile stretching across his face.

I raised my lip and clenched my fists. He stared and then twitched his head back and forth and shouted, "Your teeth are like bleached tombstones!" He smiled like he'd said the cleverest compliment.

"Now why would you say that?" Detherwheel said, turning towards the imposter.

"Why wouldn't I? Are my teeth so white? Teeth like these are a strange thing. I miss my trash!" The imposter buried his face in his hands and sobbed.

"How did I come to be here? Last I knew I was being torn apart both physically and mentally by some bloody monsters," I said.

"I told you not to move," Detherwheel said, jumping from the desk and onto the couch's arm.

"The Seething," the imposter said.

"The what?"

"The Seething. They are foul beasts that rot a man's soul. Thankfully I haven't one, but boy would I be afraid if I did!"

"I don't believe in such nonsense," I said, crossing my arms. "But that doesn't explain how I ended up here."

"How do we all?" he said.

Detherwheel cackled like the imposter had told a joke. "How much further must we travel in this skull-planet? There are many more wells to explore." Detherwheel tapped his tail impatiently and frowned.

"How are you feeling?" the imposter said, leaning forward and resting his elbows on the desk. With his hands folded in front of him and his eyebrows furrowed, he made for a poor image of a therapist.

It was odd, really. I'd started to forget that the imposter looked exactly me. For that matter, I hadn't seen my reflection in god knew how long. This quest of mine seemed to be taking place outside any semblance of time. Detherwheel harrumphed at being ignored, and I sat up attentively on the couch, trying to mirror the imposter's pose.

"What's your name?" I said.

"You've been thinking of me as an imposter, so just keep going with that."

I frowned. Could he read my thoughts?

Yes I can.

I didn't even bother acting surprised. At least he looked like me. I drew my eyebrows further down and stared at the imposter in his dead eyes.

You seem to have forgotten Bog.

"I don't need Bog."

Do you not wonder what's become of him? Do you not even think of his silence?

"I think of Sixela." I scowled and beat at my aching chest. "I don't need a spider trapping me anymore."

We are all trapped in the spider's web. Most try to ignore it. But to ignore it is to do nothing, and to do nothing is the worst of all sins.

"I don't need your useless sins. I don't need this harebrained attempt at therapy. Go back to being vermin, you're no good at being me."

The imposter stood up and smiled. "Perhaps you're better at being vermin yourself. No matter, an associate of mine will speak to you first. Then you may proceed."

A subtle ticking noise leaked out from under the desk.

"What is that! And where must we go to continue the quest?" Detherwheel shouted, turning a sickly purplish hue.

"I didn't know you could change colors," I said.

"My colors! My colors! Oh, what is becoming of me. Curse Sixela for forcing me to do this task!"

Detherwheel's body flashed in a rainbow ripple of colors. Finally, he returned to his normal vibrant green after some violent hyperventilation.

The ticking is a bomb under my desk. It will blow you all up in a bit. But first, you must speak with my associate. Try not to pay the ticking any mind.

The imposter winked and backed into the garish yellow wallpaper behind him and vanished. Little forks and knives ran up and down the walls in a comically juvenile fashion. I didn't even care to notice the imposter's disappearance; the hideous walls had attracted all my attention. I stared at the wall until my eyes stung. I yawned and turned to Detherwheel. I figured I'd keep the bit about the bomb to myself. Perks of knowing thyself, I guess. Even if thyself was vermin.

Earlier I had grown tired of this game, this quest… but now after the Seething had struck me, I felt furious at the prospect of leaving it unfinished. And Sixela. Her beauty still made me flush. Leaning back on the couch, I crossed my arms and waited for the associate to arrive.

A giant human ear hovered out of the wallpaper. The ear was the same size as me and had a giant mouth with bright red lips and blazing white teeth. The ear hovered above the chair as if sitting, and smiled. I didn't know how the thing could possibly hear on account of its ear canal being blocked by that whorish smirk it wore. And the inside of the ear was flat with no cartilage. I only assumed it was an ear because it looked like skin and was ear-shaped.

"Can you hear me?" I asked.

Detherwheel squeaked, falling onto his back in a fit of uncontrollable laughter.

"The spider spun evil, and he called it good," the ear said in a shrieking whisper, like wind storming through a burning forest.

I coughed and rubbed at my chest. I could feel something crawling deeper, burrowing inside my heart. Was it Bog? Was it the aftermath of the Seething? I was sure Bog was still in there somewhere, remaining silent.

"You can't call good evil. That is impossible," I managed to croak.

"Evil is the nothing. And there once was nothing and the spider. And then nothing became something. So, evil became good. For if evil is nothingness—non-being—then because all who live are being, once they pass into eternity the non-being of their evil will perish, leaving only the good of their true selves. The poison of the spider kills evil and brings about the true image in every creature caught in the spider's web that ever was or will be."

"What is this nonsense! Let us move on with our quest!" Detherwheel shouted.

"The nothing is our choice! The nothing is an abstraction! It never was and it never is. Evil exists when we choose to not exist by not being ourselves!" I shouted, a sudden burst of passion and clarity lighting up my mind.

"Evil exists in nonexistence. Does the spider's reach not touch all aspects of reality and unreality?" The ear's whisper raised in pitch, like air blown into a glass bottle.

"The spider? The spider! Do you mean the creator? Is that how you play this? I'm not going to blame some abstract creator for my own ills! I choose! I have chosen! Now leave me be!" I shouted, standing up and lurching forward as I gripped the desk, ready to hurl the hunk of wood out of my way.

"But the choice had to come from something," the ear murmured.

"I thought it was a nothing." I settled myself down and fell back onto the couch, chuckling at this absurdity. The bomb's ticking seemed to be speeding up. "Doesn't this all seem a bit superfluous, with a bomb ticking away to our deaths?" I said.

"A bomb!" Detherwheel shrieked, climbing on my back and cowering, his head just barely peeking over my shoulder.

"Let's go!" I shouted, running around the desk and straight at the hideous wallpaper.

The ear smiled as my surroundings quivered like gelatin, and suddenly, Detherwheel and I stumbled into a fanciful banquet hall.

A mass of blubbering fat sat at the head of a long table. The monstrosity was the color of watered-down orange juice left out too long. It had no other noticeable features, just rolls and rolls of fat. Food was disappearing into the folds of skin, and two short stubby arms groped at the piles of food towering on several plates that were all apparently for this useless looking pile of chewed bubblegum.

"Eat! Eat!" the talking blob shouted, his words gurgling as if emerging from a pit of sludge.

The food's smell was overbearingly rich, so pleasant and strong that my mouth immediately watered. Licking my lips, I sat down on the other side of the table in the only empty chair. Only then did I realize who else was sitting at the table. At every chair, a bleached white skeleton was seated with empty plates in front of each of them. Their jaws were unhinged in a permanently broken frown.

"Another ugly one joins my table!" the blob said, pointing his meaty hands at me. The skeletons all turned to me at once. I hadn't realized they were alive.

"If I may ask, how can you consider me ugly? You don't even have eyes to see," I said.

"But I have food to taste."

"I can see that."

"Delicious! You're just as bony as the rest of this lot. I'm as round as the lovely skull-planet and without the bones!"

The closest skeleton to my left nudged me with his arm. His hand was surprisingly warm. "We weren't always this thin. But that blob over there takes all our food."

"Why don't you take it back?" I asked.

The skeleton laughed so hard that his neck snapped forward and his skull landed in the center of his empty plate with his empty eye sockets aimed directly at me.

"Aren't we all bones and nothing but?" the detached skull said, bouncing up and down on the plate.

"Then I'm nothing but!" the blob burst out. A throaty guffaw trumpeted from all his folds of flesh at once.

The skeletons burst into a clattering laughter, clicking and bouncing so hard that all of them had their skulls detached. And just like the skeleton who'd first lost his head, they all ended up with their skulls on their empty plates—all of their sockets gazing at me. I itched at my neck and tried to play it cool, but I knew I wasn't convincing. Perhaps the most frightening part was that even the blob had ceased its incessant eating and was just sitting there. I cleared my throat in an attempt to break the sudden silence.

"Tell a story!" Detherwheel said, dancing on my shoulder. I gave a start, forgetting that the lizard was still there.

The detached skulls turned away from me and bounced on their plates, clamoring for a story.

"All right, all right. Story time it is," the blob said.

I sighed, relieved that everyone had stopped looking at me. I nodded gratefully at Detherwheel, and he winked at me.

"I'm going to tell you a truly great story. There once was a man who found the perfect hiding place. It was a fortress, desolate and forgotten on some distant island. The fortress had walls, oh so tall. The fortress had dungeons, oh so deep. The man hid in the deepest depths of the fortress. He had found his perfect hiding place. At the same time, the hiding man had left behind his once beloved friend. This friend searched in vain for the hiding man. The friend managed to find the fortress, but he could not figure out how to scale its oh so tall walls. The friend settled outside the fortress and began to build his own. Only, his fortress was not a fortress but a kingdom. A lovely town sprouted out from the friend's economic brilliance, while the forgotten fortress lay in disrepair on the other side of the island. The town grew and grew until it reached the fortress's walls. The friend, now an old man and the unquestioned king of his kingdom, looked sadly at the fortress, remembering his hiding friend. But what I have failed to tell you is this: both these men were tasked with finding the perfect hiding place. The friend forgot this task. The hiding man did not. And as the friend's kingdom grew, storm clouds gathered and blew away the city and its king as if they never were there. The hiding man continued hiding, waiting for his next command."

As the blob finished its story, it suddenly froze in place like unmolded clay. All the skulls in their dinner plates stared silently at me. The skeleton's body beside me tapped my shoulder. The skeleton gestured at its skull that was still resting on the dinner plate.

"Listen to your heart's beating," it said to me.

I took a deep breath. I was petrified at this abrupt and unwelcome stillness. My heart sped up as if anxious at my sudden attention.

"Listen past its beating and feel that terrible, hollow ache. Feel the shallow plunge of the dagger—to remove it would be to destroy."

I took several deeper breaths. The skull was right; there was a strange heaviness in my chest that was hollow and close. It was a kind of pain that somehow went deeper than physical in its shallowness.

"You can bury the dagger with anger. You can bury it by acknowledging it. But to get rid of it—that requires a deft hand that nobody possesses. To notice it is to begin. To remove it is the end. The problem and solution are this: the beginning and the end must come in a moment, at once."

I frowned and shook my head, filling myself with rage until my chest was forgotten. This quest, these monsters were not real. I was insane. I was insane.

"I'm mad!" I shouted, laughing at my insanity. "Nothing is real! None of this is!" I shouted louder.

The skulls rolled backwards all at once and clattered to the floor. The upright, headless skeletons broke apart at the same time as if whatever had been holding them aloft had suddenly snapped. I pounded my fist on the table and grabbed the skull who had spoken to me and hurtled it at the unmoving blob. The skull disappeared into the blob's flesh. The blob jiggled before collapsing into a rotten smelling yellowish liquid that was filled with chunks like spoiled milk.

Breathing slower, I sighed and tried to regain some semblance of control. A gloom gripped me, and I closed my eyes trying to wish away this sudden nightmare. Everything seemed so unclear. Nothing made sense. There was no connection from one thing to the next. I withdrew further into my mind, searching for that abyss of nothingness. Images of Sixela's body bloomed in a rush of rainbow-like colors, her figure shimmering in front of me. I reached out for the image but my being was gone, only she was there in the dark. I smiled. The thought of her was keeping me alive. Yet… a darker thought intruded my peace. Was a delusion

worth surviving for?

I opened my eyes to find the banquet hall empty. A fine

layer of dust covered the tables and chairs. The blob and the

skeletons had simply vanished. I scratched my back and sat up

with a start, my heart racing as I came back to myself.

"Detherwheel… what is happening," I whispered, afraid of

the silence.

I got no answer. I looked at both my shoulders and felt

around my shirt, but he was gone. The lizard was gone. I was

alone.

"Hello?" I called out, my voice cumbersome in the dusty

quiet.

I tried to imagine Sixela again but couldn't conjure up a

clear image in my mind. All that I could see when I closed my eyes

was blackness. When I opened them, the room was more decrepit

than before. Several chairs were collapsed on the floor. The dust

had increased to the point of layering everything in an off-white

hue. I looked down at myself and yelped. I was covered in the same amount of dust. How long had I been here? How long was I

alone? My eyes darted around the walls, looking for a way out but

there were no doors. Off in the corner I spotted something… a

small square window covered with rotting yellow curtains.

I stumbled out of my chair which collapsed behind me in a

cloud of ash, and made my way to the curtained windows, my legs

wobbly and weak. My breathing was heavy and I felt ready to pass

out. I yanked the hole-ridden cloth from the windows and got

showered with dust and filth. Wiping my eyes, I caught a glimpse

of my hands and staggered backwards. My hands were wrinkled

and liver spotted, my fingernails black and long. I felt my face and

yelled, my voice frail and shaky. I was a mess of sagging skin

overrun with wrinkles. I rubbed my scalp and felt nothing but

scabbed and hairless skin. How long had I been here?

A gentle, light sound of flittering laughter fluttered through

the window. With labored breathing, I tried to wipe the dirt

covered glass but was unable to see through it. The laughter

continued to rise and fall, angelic in its gaiety. The laughter of

children. That was what I was hearing. I was surprised that I could hear at all, the way the rest of my body seemed to be so broken down.

The window refused to budge and I fell to the ground, my back against the wall and my face buried in my hands. I was afraid to look up at the room again but couldn't resist. I slowly rose my head and blinked open my eyes. The table was split down the center and nothing else remained. I looked at my hands and saw nothing but bone. The skin was gone. I felt my face, already knowing what would be there. I was nothing but bone now.

This was the lot I had chosen. This was what my desperation for Sixela had wrought. I'd closed myself off from the world in hopes of being handed heaven. Now I had neither. My hiding place was myself, and I couldn't even command me. There was nothing. Nothing. I... what remained of me... felt like nothing. My bones ached dully, but I could no longer hear. And then... now I couldn't see. It finally seemed like I could rest. I was empty now. Empty. I blinked, or imagined that I did so. Once. Then another time. I wanted to rest. It would be so easy to remain. I stood up, now nothing but an aching skeleton. I didn't care. I didn't care if I couldn't see or breathe or hear. I wouldn't stay here. I wouldn't!

I groped in the darkness, reaching for the glass of the window. I struck the glass with all my might, again and again until shards of it shattered onto the ground along with fragments of my bones. I climbed up on the window sill and thrust myself forward. I felt nothing as I fell and crashed into the ground, my bones scattering everywhere. I felt nothing. I saw nothing. It was only black. I belonged to the abyss now.

Chapter 4

Skin

A designed wilderness surrounded me in elaborate, mazelike waves of barely contained greenery. Voluptuous trees lined grassy paths that were dotted with every color of flower. I was in the perfect garden. The countless kinds of plants seemed to thrive without having to compete for resources or space.

The colors saturated the landscape so ethereally that a glowing mist seemed to shudder through everything as if the colors were too bright for the naked eye. I looked up to see a clear sky, pearl-blue, clean, and inviting. There was no sun, but it was brighter than day. Birds chirped in a calm cacophony of melodies—an ordered chaos that sounded independent and natural as well as symphonic and masterful. Everything seemed to be singing softly.

I breathed deeply. The air was thick with a welcome dew that exuded life and calm. Scents that could only be described as life itself came to me and I sniffed greedily. Fresh. Alive. No decay. That was the smell of this paradise. I sighed, the memory of the gluttonous eternal banquet leaving my mind in the calm of this place. I sighed again.

My clothes were gone. Checking my hands, I was pleased to see them back to their smooth and lovely selves. I was me again, if me was the I that I currently was. Who was the old man that I'd been, and where did he go to? There was no sign of the window I'd leapt from either. The lush garden spread as far as I could see in all directions. The grassy paths snaked through the controlled density of the foliage, branching all around like roots of a tree.

Not caring about my nakedness or what I looked like, I smiled, spun in a circle, and started walking in the direction my body teetered. I reached and picked a luscious fruit that hung over the path I was on. The plum's rich red color was a deep, bright purplish hue that shimmered in an enticing way as if begging to be picked. The taste was not overwhelming but a perfect balance of tanginess, tartness, and sweetness that mingled on my tongue pleasantly after I'd finished eating the fruit.

The sudden harsh sound of manual labor rang out shrilly against the gentle quietness of the garden. The banging of a hammer on metal got louder as I rounded the corner of the path I followed. The hammer then took on a chimelike sound that increased in amplitude, melody, and harmony, and decreased in harshness and dissonance the closer I got. The hammer was beginning to sound like the continuous plucking of a somber harp string.

At last I managed to find the source of the strange sound. The garden had widened into a large meadow of sunflowers with a small stone hut directly in the middle of the field. The sunflowers spiraled out from the house like rays of sunlight. From the slightly elevated path I still stood on, I could make out a hunched figure in a dark cloak banging away at an anvil.

I pushed through the sunflowers, a frantic sense of urgency overtaking me. The sunflowers refused to bend and they pushed back. Vines grabbed my ankles and I tumbled to the ground, my scream ruining the melody of the garden and the anvil. The sunflowers whipped their heads down and struck me as their vines cut off the circulation in my legs. Sprawled on my back, I stared through the sunflowers' billowing petals and at the sunless and pure sky. A shadowed figure soared through the air with its silhouette stretched out as if flying.

It was the cloaked figure! The stranger landed with grace, the cloak billowing and flapping like wings of an archangel. The stranger hopped rapidly about and sliced through the vines with a buzzing dagger that collapsed the sunflowers like a poisonous sting. The flowers were not being severed but stung by the strange dagger as they drooped in paralysis. I could hardly glimpse the dagger the stranger moved so quickly. It appeared to be shrouded in a red-orange shadow that crackled like fire.

The strange figure wielding the weapon remained an enigma. He was flipping about and making short work of the ferocious sunflowers, but his body and face remained covered. At last, after an astounding double flip, the cloak's hood fell back as the stranger struck the last of the whipping sunflowers in an acrobatic flourish. It was a frog—a frog that stood upright like a human, even with its severe hunch.

"Come with me. Come with me," it said. "My name is Cherub. You must understand that these flowers are the terrible price of paradise. It takes a certain kind to walk through untouched. Not always a good kind, yes?" Cherub spoke in a throaty gurgle, spitting words out with a ferocious haste as if he were afraid of losing his speech.

His cold arms enveloped me, and he carried me like a child to his hut in the clearing. The sunflowers bowed to him as he made his way through. I shivered; his skin was slimy and clammy, and I was relieved when he finally put me down beside his anvil. I rubbed at my ankles and sat there. He blinked and stared with his hood pulled back, and I tried my best not to gape too openly. A human-sized frog. A talking, warrior-blacksmith frog at that! Named Cherub too! I wanted to laugh, but instead I shook my head and tried to think.

"What makes the sunflowers serve and not strike? Why do they not harm you?" I asked, pulling my knees to my bare chest.

Cherub hopped over to me and sat down like a frog is supposed to. I smiled as he squinted his eyes at me in contemplation.

"Only one who is nothing can serve and be served, so far nothing that nothing is not nothing enough. To acknowledge this, is to become someone and a something."

I lowered my head and frowned, gripping my knees tighter. The peace of the garden seemed cracked, broken in the suffering I'd faced. Was the Seething still inside me? Was I still possessed by my desire for Sixela? Was I simply contriving all of this nonsense merely to feel meaning at my stumbling to survive? I could never become nothing when there was always something dragging me away. Away and towards… I didn't know. I ran my hands through my hair and pulled back, too perplexed and muddled to make any sense of this nonsense.

Apparently noticing my distress, Cherub pointed at his anvil. On the anvil was a silver pike that was incredibly thin, like a strand of hair, but twice my height in length. There was a makeshift hammer of wood and stone on the ground beside the anvil.

Cherub slowly stood and walked to the anvil. He lifted the spear and held it preciously, eyeing its shimmering metal in the glare of the empty sky.

"I'm making my spear to catch the golden four-winged flying fish. The problem is, it refuses to fly and use its wings! It's hunkered down in the mire of my pond. It's as tiny as a gnat, and the only one of its kind. To catch it, is to bring about the end."

"But why is your spear so thin?" I said.

"It is up to me to catch it. But with a spear so fine, time will tell me when my time is. Until that time, I work on perfecting it. When not working, I stare fearfully into the face of this black pond, wondering when it will be our time."

"Is the pond nearby?"

"The pond is."

"You said our?" I said.

"Yes," Cherub said, nodding. He put the spear down gently on the anvil and pointed at his hut. "He sits in there on his wooden throne. His name is Seraph and he hasn't spoken or moved for eleven years. He is the closest to Power."

"Power? What do you mean?"

"Ask him yourself." Cherub unceremoniously flung the door open and I swallowed, following fearfully behind.

A white sheep with black spots splotched on its wool sat in a chair, slumped and unmoving. The sheep's eyes were vacant and glossed over, appearing to stare at the wall but really not seeming to see at all.

"Seraph?" I whispered.

Nothing. No reaction. Seraph sat there. I stepped slightly closer and looked at his face. He had an odd shaped black splotch above his mouth which comically made him look like he had a walrus-like mustache.

"Caiaphas was put in chains by Seraph. This sheep is a god." Cherub hung his head in reverence, drawing his hood to cover his face.

"A god?"

"He was crucified with madness."

"A god?" I repeated with a shake of my head.

"You too! You too! You must be divine! A fool is all the wiser. A madman is sane."

"I need to get going."

I backed out of the room and ran. I crashed through the sunflowers in a random direction. They put up no resistance this time around. I might have imagined it, but the seemed to just ignore me as if I were nothing. Nevertheless, I was grateful for the respite. The cult back there was too much. I didn't hear any signs of pursuit at the very least.

As I jogged through the outer rim of sunflowers, I stumbled onto a grassy slope and rolled down an unseen hill. I kept rolling and rolling, bouncing about like a rubber ball. My mad descent finally ended with a splash. I'd tumbled onto a pebbly beach. Groaning, I got to my feet and examined my body for what I expected to be ghastly wounds. Nothing. My skin looked somehow healthier than it had ever been. I still ached though. The pain sloshed inside my bones like lava; I felt as though I were on fire. It was the kind of hot prickly pain that made you pull your hand back from the stove. I couldn't pull myself back from myself!

I shuddered at the thought. I held my hands up in front of my face and examined them with detachment. An uneasy feeling arose; the hands were my hands but my thoughts didn't feel anchored in whatever reality those hands were in. My mind tremored, the more I thought the less grounded in reality I was. The surroundings seemed unreal. Most frightfully of all—I didn't feel real. I'd had this kind of depersonalization before, but never to such an extreme as this. It was as if my thoughts were trying to leave existence behind. In a sense, I had ceased to exist, at least in my subjective experience. My thoughts spiraled out of my body like smoke through a chimney. I was still a body, but nothing was real. I wasn't real.

No longer truly myself, I wasn't an I, but a ghost; a specter spectating my body and thoughts. No me. As not me, I tried to cling to whatever falsity I could convince myself of in this body and this world. Accepting the falsity of me, and the falsity of reality by believing in another, I managed to calm myself down. I was still disoriented, but at least I could move about.

Taking a couple of drawn out breaths, trying to reconnect my thoughts to my body, I looked at the lake in front of me. Or was it an ocean? There were no waves, just gentle waters lapping refreshingly at my feet. Good waves for ants. I couldn't help but picture Detherwheel trying to surf these ripples. Even he might be too large for that. I wondered where the lizard had gone off to? He'd probably gone to Sixela to inform her of my failure. But I was still here, still going as patient and longsuffering as ever. If she didn't wait for me, I could still hope to finish and wait for her.

Sighing, I sat down on the pebbles and let the water gather around me. It was cold, but the soothing kind of cold. It had been a long day…or year…or century? Honestly it was hard to tell with the banquet fiasco. It could have been millennia, or even an eternity. Was this the afterlife? If so, I wasn't a fan. It was awfully lonely and the characters I met were all insane. I yawned and stretched onto my back, the water covering me in a half-finished burial.

"Insane," I muttered. I was going to try and start enjoying this if I was going to be stuck here forever.

"Who are you calling insane?" a voice dinged. Moocha peered worriedly at my face, casting her shadow over my sprawled-out form.

I squinted at her. "What happened to your bell head? Now you've got a silly silver triangle for a head! I guess it sounds better than that rusty thing from before."

Moocha shook her head. A delightful and timid ting sounded each time she moved in the slightest. "I was the mooiest bell-cow. Now I'm the mooiest of all cows. The trooiest too!"

Not wanting to leave the comfort of the tickling water, I closed my eyes and sighed. I could feel her presence just as much as I could hear it… and smell it too. I smiled. Rich chocolate, so fragrant that I could taste it simply with my nostrils. That was one way to bring me back into myself, experiencing such a joyful sense.

"Where have you been?" I said, my eyes closed and voice distant.

"You ask where I've been, but have you not thought to inquire about your spider?" Each word she spoke raised to a higher note that became more delicate and beautiful as she went on.

"Bog? Bog?" I slurred, opening my eyes in surprise confusion. I frowned. "He's not my spider. But he abandoned me to this quest, to my desires, to my suffering and to myself."

"A spider does not abandon. A spider keeps its victims close."

"Am I a victim?" I said.

Water covered my face and I started choking as I was suddenly submerged. I blindly reached out for Moocha's neck. Feeling the warmth of her fur, I hugged her neck and she lifted me out of the water and to my feet.

"Are you?" Moocha said, her ringing a sudden sharp and harsh alarm.

Surprised at myself, I hugged her tight and took in her warm and sweet scent. With my head buried on her shoulder and nuzzled against her fur, I whispered, "I'm alone." I wept.

She gently chimed a lullaby-like melody as her fur absorbed my tears. "We are only victims of ourselves. To be a victim of a spider, one first must be caught. One must then surrender," she dinged soothingly.

A humming from the lake joined her with cherubic chiming. The sounds arose to a rapturous fever pitch. I felt anew. I smiled at Moocha, patted her back, and gazed at the symphonic lake still harking aloud like a perfectly tuned orchestra—an angelic choir.

"A moment awaits. A boat to row you forever in the now. Do not look back, because looking forward is looking at forever which might as well be this moment. And now, the moment arrives." Moocha's ringing lowered in volume until it sounded as if it were my own thoughts.

I didn't need to look behind me to know that Moocha was gone. The lake abruptly stopped singing and all was quiet but for the sloshing of the water. Then, as if materializing from the water itself, a rowboat glided towards me. A spindly man with a more wide than tall black top hat calmly rowed. As the boat neared, the figure before me remained stooped and casual, rowing as if not knowing he was about to strike land. He wore a high collared peacoat and his hair tumbled out his hat in wild blonde locks.

A feeling of intense, fearful passion arose inside me and it was all I could do to keep myself from running the other way. I swallowed and smiled, wading out into the water. I feared not getting into the boat more than the uncertainty of enjoining myself to such a strange enterprise. The boat teetered and swayed as I heaved myself aboard. Yet, the rower kept on rowing, still headed towards land. As I was about to warn him, I fell back and yelped with a start. The shore was gone. Endless water surrounded us, or at least that's what I could only assume. A heavy fog had descended over the surrounding waters like a murder of crows feasting on a carcass. Only the rowboat remained untouched by this impenetrable fog.

I peered at the rowing man's face. He had gentle yet passionate features; his crystalline eyes were fixed on the bottom of the rowboat. Almost angelic, he was a strikingly pretty man. I coughed, but he remained staring at whatever it was he was staring at.

"Don't you know where it is you're heading?" I said. He remained silent and rowing so I tried again. "Don't you need to look?"

"I'm not looking where I'm going because I'm already there, or always going there. I don't need to look because what isn't yet, isn't ever. There is only this eternal instant, which is right now and always right now. I'm going where I am not, but am." His eyes connected with mine, his blue irises drowning me with intensity. His eyes were loud, yet his voice was as calm and quiet as the lake.

The sloshing of his ancient, sea-stained wooden oars droned constantly in the background like the ticking of a grandfather clock. I hoped there wouldn't be an alarm.

"Why do you row?" I asked, not understanding what he was getting at in the slightest.

The man grinned. His entire body seemed to smile as he sat up straighter, still rowing at the same pace. "I row because to not row, is to not be. Rowing is a faith in itself. To not row is to not have faith, and to not have faith is to not be yourself. Rowing without looking is simply seeing what is already there, what is already me. I know that time is what it is. I know that I am privy to decay. I know this. But it is my unseeing rowing that brings me to now. This moment is a now, but it is much more when free in the infinite."

I rubbed my eyebrow and attempted to recline as comfortably as I could in what little space there was for me in the rowboat.

"I prefer my eyesight." I said.

"And what if you lose that?"

"I prefer my mind. If I lost that, I wouldn't be alive, now would I?" I shook my head. This man sounded like a fool. Blind faith was something I refused to entertain, especially with how quixotic the man's dialectics were. Reason must prevail.

"Reason is unreason. Please." He laughed and I crossed my arms self-consciously. I hadn't said that last bit aloud. "We *try* to live by reason. Is it reasonable to suffer living when everything eventually ends, all emotion and meaning forgotten and dissolved into nothingness? Struggle for struggle's sake is a nice lie we tell ourselves to keep us going. That's just our biology lying! Are you reasonable for loving a specter that in all likelihood is just a figment of your imagination? Reason. Yes, very reasonable indeed." He finished his spiel with a guttural laughing fit that was unbecoming of his gentle voice.

"I refuse to be blind." I frowned at the madman and pulled my arms to my chest in a vicelike grip.

"Any way we look, we are blind. The finite cannot gaze into the infinite. And the finite gazing at the finite, ends in blindness—the black endless nothingness of the eternal abyss. Instead of succumbing to the abyss, instead of gazing stubbornly at it, I leap over it. The other side is just as uncertain. Yet I leap to it. That is why I row. That is where I am and am going. It is who I am. Without it, there is no me or you, or truly anyone at all." The man had returned to his determined rowing, staring once more at the bottom of the boat.

"What is your name?" I asked, my voice shaking. I could sense an uneasy shifting in the air. The fog surrounding us seemed to be pressing into our space, running against the edge of the boat with tendril-like talons eerily scraping away.

"Graveyard."

All at once, his face melted away. A skeleton was all that remained of him, yet he kept rowing. The fog pounced on his bones and covered me in a complete and colorless gray. I felt as though I were dissolving, and once more—darkness enveloped me.

Chapter 5

Ikon

Rubbing my eyes, the darkness foggily swirled into a jumble of bright surroundings. I was in a thick jungle with muggy and rotten air. I sighed. This whole game was ridiculously tiresome and dross. Nobody was worth this insanity, not even Sixela. My own life wasn't worth living if I had to keep playing this game.

"Then don't play it," a soothing voice drawled from above. Smoke clouds drifted down from the trees and I coughed violently. "You are free to leave whenever."

The voice was in the canopy of leaves above me. I couldn't see much up there other than descending tendrils of gray smoke.

"How do I stop this madness?" I said, trying to see through the billowing puffs of gray assaulting my senses.

"You must be king. A different kind that is. A king without a kingdom. The only subject is yourself alone, for all a man can know is himself. An infinite chasm separates us all. We think we understand the glowing eyes of the multitude, but the light we see is a reflection of the selves we imagine. You and all, are alone."

A bluish-black chameleon emerged from the smoke, hanging there on the tree limb while puffing away at a cigarette dangling from its mouth. One of its eyes was listless and askew as if it were made of glass. The other eye stared directly at me and I hunched my shoulders.

"I devour the flies others surround themselves with. I eat through the chains of the many, so that the lonely may come forth in absolute freedom, proclaiming their truths. The gaze of the other is the judge, the executioner of Hell. Blot out the glowing lies, swallow the darkness and taste the flies."

"I'm not hungry. I'm simply bored." I squared my shoulders and breathed deep, inhaling the smoke as if to dare the chameleon to say more.

"You are inauthentic. You act as you do because you believe that which you worship is watching. Even if she is, you should not do what she says for her sake. Your faith in her is pathetic—a chain to the glowing eyes of the deceived and enslaved multitude. You are not free."

"Why should I listen to you?"

"Because I'm telling you to be you. The spider of yours tried to make you be him."

I smiled. I thought back to the rower, and then to Moocha and what she said of Bog. "What if the only way to be myself is to recognize myself with myself, connected by the spider's web and to the spider himself? We are alone, it's true. But when we are wriggling in the grip of death, that is—life; the spider's dripping fangs do not pierce these flies you speak of, but the fangs break the hardened shell of the chasm that seperates until we are all connected together. Perhaps this loneliness is only a step to be climbed. Perhaps you hide in your swarms of flies, eating your fill yet refusing to give an inch to the great other."

"You speak in riddles like the rower. The rower is a religious fool. He speaks of blind freedom. My eye is open."

I laughed. "At least he is moving forever. You just sit there in imagined freedom."

The chameleon puffed harder. "You are deceived and refuse to leave the comfort of the collective whole. It is your loss. Your deception."

"Why do you cling to that tree? Are you incapable of freeing yourself from such a weak limb? Building your thought on such frailty is doomed to fail. The tree will wither. Your thinking is trapped in the past… the finite consumes it. I live in the forever moment. The rower helped me see that."

"The rower is stuck rowing. I speak from myself," the chameleon said. Smiling, he spit his cigarette on top of my head. I furiously flicked it away. He coughed and continued, "I'll stay here and burn with my truth. You melt in the heat of your lies. If you choose to stay a slave to the spider, you will never be free."

"And are you? Or are you a slave to your decaying self?" I said. Flames abruptly burst from the discarded cigarette, engulfing the green surroundings in a bright red glow. I held my ground. "The only freedom that exists is in captivity of the spider. The spider is the infinite. How can you be free if you are finite?"

"Your truth. Your lie. The infinite is imagined." The chameleon scowled and disappeared in the bloodlike light of fire.

I took a deep breath and turned away. I walked through the burning jungle as if the flames were incapable of touching me. Of course, I was sorely wrong and after some glowing embers licked the nape of my neck, I set off running. The pulsating light and heat of the jungle encircled me. It seemed as though I was in a forest of eternal flame. I wasn't sure why, but I couldn't remember what the jungle looked like when it was whole. The flames had somehow burnt a hole in my memory.

With choked breath, I sprinted blindly forward, hoping against all hopes that I'd escape this burning death. As I ran, I felt a sudden plop on my shoulder. Despite my smoldering surroundings and the noxious fumes of the forest, I grinned. Detherwheel had returned! He clung to my shoulder like he'd never left.

"Run! Keep going! This burning forest is not for you," Detherwheel cried.

Detherwheel beat at my back with his tail and I laughed, sprinting even harder. I was not alone. I had my purpose. Only, I didn't think Sixela was my purpose anymore. I had an overwhelming sense that I needed to keep pushing, that I might stumble into Bog's embrace. I realized right then and there, as I choked through the ashes, the spider did love. Bog was mine, and I was his. I wasn't alone as the chameleon claimed. I wasn't filled with hate, even as the Seething still swarmed in the depths of myself. I understood now that this was my moment. I was rowing as I ran. Graveyard and I were together. I was not alone. The spider loves.

"The spider loves!" I shouted.

Detherwheel giggled on my shoulder. "Sixela does too, but that is no matter for now. Escape the flames! Run!" His shouting was shrill, but oddly comforting. I missed his constant quipping.

I ran. The heat seemed to lose its touch. The fire bloomed, its flames flowering around me into a tunnel. The angry red of the inferno softened—orange then yellow, yellow then white. The flames ceased dancing and all at once they froze into an icy blue, unmoving and seemingly sculpted of snow. I was now in an endless tunnel of tundra. No trees. No life. Just frozen white-marble flame. And cold. I couldn't remember the warmth. It was as if I had been running in this endless tunnel of ice the whole time, the flaming forest nothing but a fever dream.

I wished I had clothes. This was no paradise. I shivered, hugging myself and standing there unable to move. Detherwheel seemed untouched by the cold. He tilted his head, blinked at me and smiled oddly as if holding in some joyous and secretive joke.

"Are you not c-cold? What is happening?" I said with my jaw clenched and my teeth chattering.

"The flames have cooled because a greater flame is coming. I told you, Sixela loves. She loves her warmth."

My heart beat and my chest flushed. Wringing my hands, the cold was forgotten. Sixela! Sixela! The spider could wait!

"Where is she?" I cried.

Detherwheel's grin grew greater at my excitement. "Don't look at me. Look behind you."

I spun around only to realize that behind me was also in front of me. The tunnel of frozen flame was now a white nothingness—an expanse surrounding me from above, below, and in every direction. My feet stood on something solid, something unseen. But from all appearances, I was perched on a great nothing, surrounded by a white nothing. This was not the black abyss of nothingness I'd experienced so many times before. This nothing… this nothing was filled with desire and excitement—an encompassing energy that exuded from myself and the expanse around me. This was a desire so strong that I trembled anxiously at it remaining unfulfilled. This was an energy and libido hotly suspended in perpetual lust, unable to be abated. I panted like a deprived, thirsting animal and dropped to me knees in a hopeless attempt at surrendering to this force within me and without me. Detherwheel dropped from my shoulder and bowed.

Like a god, no… not like but simply as—as a true goddess, Sixela appeared. The myth that was Aphrodite cowered in the shadow of Sixela's glory. No goddess from any mythology could compare. Sixela stood before me, radiant and glowing with a sun-drenched splendor. Her transparency from the park was gone; she had become realer than reality itself. A robe hung around her waist, flaring out and flashing bursts of shapely legs. The desire within and without pounded and pulsed, stabbing my mind with ecstatic crescendos of shivering pleasure.

Her torso was bare, supple and ripe, full and rapturous. Too perfect for any grotesque and grasping hands. Too perfect for my clumsily worded descriptions. Her stomach was flat and toned, and the robe dangled just low enough to reveal sensually carved lines sloping downwards to hint at an unthinkable treasure buried beneath the white cloth. Even her navel was heavenly, a perfect circle open and unblinking, gently lipped like a sleepy eye.

Finally, with a desperate and shameful fervor I drank in the beauty of her face. Her eyes were lightning breathed opals—pristine sky colored icily with the essence of soul—the essence of life thundering there in her diamond blue stare. The structure of her face was strong yet feminine, carved of stone yet softened with a honey-like fluidity. Her cheeks were more prominent and pristine than Prophet Elias. Her nose divinely flowed down and outwards, powerful and commanding, unapologetically long and sharp, and still beautiful and godly in its shape and form.

Her lips were strong and luscious, two wings of a celestial butterfly drenched in honey—thick rose petals dripping nectar. Her salt-sprayed scent shined with sultry, succulent island aromas that I shuddered at with desire. I could taste her Edenesque smell, fresh and sweet, saccharine and sumptuous. I was mortal. Her beauty and being were eternal. I belonged to death. She belonged to beyond.

All my attempted poetic verbiage and misnomers declaring her perfect beauty collapsed under the weight of the finite grasping at the infinite. I was ash and she was star. Can a termite describe the heavens? Can an atom describe a planet? I bowed my head. To look at her longer was to debase myself of my being. I was lost in her infinity. I was becoming a nothing in the light of her everything. I was destroyed.

Then, the white nothingness of desire started to hum with voices misty and light. A haunting and sugary melody surrounded me as I knelt there in shame.

Honeyed onyx waterfalling down

Tresses more precious than any crown

Stained glass eyes, a soul's paradise

Spiritual blue, opal's jealous hue

She smiles like angel wings spread,

Lips and mouth bloom rose red

Sixela, a dream

Beauty too pristine

Opal on fire,

Scorched desire

Sixela, a dream

She's the dream

The perfection of her face

Reflecting all grace

A singing body curving melodious

The rhythm of her skin is harmonious

As the breeze giggles and fruit ripens

He breathes and prays as the sun brightens

Her silence is a siren that has syphoned his soul

He loves what he cannot have and has fallen in a hole

Make him whole

Love him Love him Love him

I knew the words were about my obsession. Did the nothingness of desire want her to love me? Could it be? Could it be possible? Could I be loved?

I crouched there in my lowliness. I was petrified to look at her again, especially after that song. The white expanse kept chanting, high pitched and feminine in the background as it repeated its song in an almost instrumental fashion—as if the words had faded into nothing but feeling. I swallowed as her overpoweringly delicate scent neared. I pressed my cheek to the floor, closing my eyes and holding my breath. To breath her air was to be given over to passion. I knew that if I drank in her beauty this close, I would never know another person the same. The rest of humanity, the rest of existence would lose all its beauty in value with the eternal glory of Sixela forever branded in my mind. She laughed, her voice a coo that ran over me like warm water. My skin broke out in goosebumps as my hair stood on end.

I am not false. I chose me. I choose those that open their eyes and see. I am not too great for you. We are too great for him.

Tears poured out from my shut eyes as her voice traveled inside of me, riding my brainwaves so synchronously that her words seemed more at home inside me than my own thoughts.

He wants you to do nothing. He wants you to stay tucked in his web, stuck for eternity while you surrender yourself to his whims. Mustn't a child leave its parent's home? Do you want to be his sheep, eating and sleeping only where he deems fit? Eat where you want. Eat what you want. My something is to take part in the nothing that is the darkness to his light. He declares himself good. He declares himself as being itself. To reject him is to reject existence. I say that to accept him, is to surrender your existence into his, forever bending to his everything, his good. I say we conquer this nothingness. I say we claim it for ourselves and die to eternity. The baby dies. The mother weeps. The children starve. Suffering. To suffer is to be. His good is evil. His good evil. When

*being itself exists in juxtaposition, can the nothingness that always
was, truly be called evil? When he declares his creation good, but
then turns and calls it evil, where does the blame lie? Was it me? I
existed before the garden. Was it Eve? She chose the evil when
faced with the tyrannical good of forever twitching in the spider's
web. We were brought from nothingness into existence. We did not
ask to be. Yet we are. But to want to return to the nothingness?
How dare we! The spider crawls out from the depths, weaving his
endless web over the sweet abyss of the darkness. We did not ask to
be, and he refuses us the release of the nothing. We must suffer
eternally. Yet we did not ask to be. He brought us into being. And
he refuses us the freedom of the great nothing. Is that good? Good
evil is the kindest name for the spider. Laugh at his goodness.
Laugh at our evil. Laugh at the hypocrisy of forcing us to exist, as
if we chose the suffering of this pathetic good evil the spider
weaves. He existed forever. The nothingness was all around him. If
there is evil, does the spider's web not touch it, even if only a
wisp? He allowed the nothingness of evil to be, and his existence
refusing to end nonexistence is the ultimate good evil. Laugh at the*

spider, break through the web. There is a something beyond the good evil. There is a something the spider clings to. That something is the truth of you. That something is me. That something is the nothing of the spider. That something is us over everything else.

I opened my eyes as her words reverberated inside my skull. She stood over me, smiling lovingly. She reached down her perfect hand and held my cheek, stroking my face with her thumb in a repeating, circular motion. Suddenly, she frowned at me and I withered under her glare, ashamed at upsetting her.

"The spider still sits inside you. You must resist. Bog! Bog! Bog!" she shouted, her voice a howling torrent of wind. She spoke from outside of my mind and the result was terrifying. I felt like she was leaving me.

"Sixela!" I cried, desperately grasping her feet.

I coughed, painfully and forcefully hacking phlegm into my hands. The coughing worsened and the phlegm turned to blood. I coughed harder and harder, my eyes squeezed shut by the force of my constant hacking. A terrible burning arose in my chest, and I let out a final, forceful cough that knocked me over onto my back. When the pain cleared and I opened my eyes, Sixela looked at me in disgust.

No! No! Blessedly, it wasn't me her hatred was directed at. No! In the pool of blood from my last cough, Bog floated there like a speck of dust. Sixela raised her foot, preparing to stomp on him, when a violent peace pierced my heart, and I knew that Bog was true. Sixela was false. I desperately reached out to try to stop him from being crushed, but I was too slow. Her bare foot stomped down into the pool of black blood and bile. There wasn't a chance Bog had survived.

I screamed. I wept. I gnashed my teeth and beat my breast. Sixela pressed her foot down harder, turning it back and forth, kneading the ground and splattering her lovely, manicured foot with splotches of blood.

"What do you say?" Sixela said to me, her foot still pressing into the puddle.

I became calm all at once. I breathed deep, three times. I remembered the moment. I remembered I was in my moment. I thought of the rower. I thought of the water covering my being as Moocha stood over me. I understood that it was I who was of dust. I understood it was I who now existed. To pretend there was a something in the nothing opposite Bog was to deny existence. Blame was pointless. We choose not to be when we dive into shadow. The spider's web was no web. The spider's web was eternity. Eternity was my moment.

"You are false," I spat.

I smiled, laughing as her foot struck my chin. As my vision faded, the last image I saw was of Detherwheel clawing at my eyes and Sixela turning her back and walking away.

Chapter 6

Au Fait

Am I free against the spider? My freedom is always

against, juxtaposed to the light. My freedom is chains jangling to

the tune of opposition. The only truly free will is the one that

weaves silk; to do this, one must choose the good. One must choose

to be. That is only found in the spider's web.

"What?" I mumbled. I rubbed the back of my head and
looked around as I sat up, only to find that I wasn't sitting but
laying on a red couch. A red couch suspended in the same white
abyss I'd just seen Bog killed in. "Bog?"

But can a human weave strands of time? Can existence be

commandeered? Can our emergence from nonexistence circle to

form an interlocked infinity sign, hovering over the face of the

waters? Is chaos the nothing? Will we return to not being? The

opposite is evil. Nothing. Yet we were nothing outside of time,

before and I pray not after. Good evil: swallowing the everything of the infinite in the ending nothingness of the finite. Without both,

we are not. We cannot.

"Who?" I said, the thoughts of this strange whisper
assaulting my mind—no deeper still, my soul. My being. My
essence. My existence. I gulped, looking around for the source of
these heavy words. "Who are you?"

You know who I am.

"Sixela!" I gasped.

I curled into a ball and feverishly looked around me. There
was nothing but the red of the couch and the white of the expanse.
My naked flesh curdled with desire. My eyes were desperate for
another taste of her. Her murder of Bog forgotten; it might as well
have been of my own doing.

You silly, silly boy. The murderer you saw was the Seething
manifest. That Sixela was you. What she said and looked like was
everything you believe and desire.

"No!" I shouted. "I did not believe her." I swallowed as my
words tailed off in an obvious lie. I didn't care to believe. I was

simply reacting in fits of passion. The realization was nothing new. I ground my teeth in weakness.

The monsters have left, but you remain empty. Will you fill it with me still?

The question took me aback. Her whispering voice had hesitated. I pulled my knees to my chin and closed my eyes, folding my head in surrender. I had no words. Whatever I'd believed or said before was forgotten. Here I was now.

"Here I am," I yelled into my knees. "Can I see you?" I whispered.

You know the answer. You prefer distance. Distance is safe. Yet distance turns reality into a dream. You prefer to be stuck in your unreality. I will honor that. From afar you can long. From afar you can imagine a bridge. There is no bridge built that crosses the ocean. Know that your distance is further still. The ocean, the bridge, the you… none of it exists on the other side.

I trembled and trapped my head between my legs. I gnashed my teeth and sobbed at the harsh truth in her words. Her

ghostly whisper was the closest communion I knew. I had ceased
to exist the moment I saw her in my distance.

*Don't stop at the ceasing. Continue to be, by living with
nothingness at your back. I do not know. I do not know. I do not
know. Where has Bog gone? Why must we hate him? Why did he
bring us to be?*

"Why here?" I muttered, thinking only of myself. "Why
this couch? Why in this empty expanse? My clothes are gone and
shame left me long ago, yet this is no paradise." I jumped from the
couch and stood, clenching my fists and searching wildly for
Sixela's beauty. "This is no paradise!"

Sixela's laughter sang inside my head. I smiled. I didn't
care if it was directed at me. I unclenched my palms and bowed my
head, closing my eyes once more.

*This is exactly your paradise. This is exactly what happens
when your muddled madness is entertained. This is your spider's
web. This is your silk sun. Your bog to sink in.*

I fell. The white abyss swallowed me. The blank expanse
scorched into a tar black, bubbling into a sweltering and burning

cold dark. Stuck in unreality, floating inside my head once more, I surprised myself as I thought of Bog. Whether or not that had been Sixela or the Seething didn't matter. I saw Bog in my blood. I saw… her—me, grounding him to dust. But he couldn't be crushed. He couldn't! The spider couldn't be crushed! Not this one. Not the one. The puddle of my blood was an empty grave. I paused, aware of where my thoughts were heading. Sixela. Sixela.

My heart jumped joyously with a stag-like longing. No matter what, there was always a reason to fall back to her. Reasons based in unreason, but reasons nonetheless. I couldn't give up the lie, regardless of whoever started it or told it. Sixela was still the Great. If this was my paradise—this cold, burning empty black, then I deserved it. This must be what I want. I breathed and let myself dissolve into the emptiness. Meaning to meaninglessness. Being to nothingness. I was—to not be.

"You cannot rest yet," Detherwheel said. His clammy tail wrapped around the nape of my neck and he poked his head at my cheek as if to kiss it. "We must increase in distance. We must finish this quest where it began. How else can one get any farther?"

His piping voice shattered my dissolution. The pieces of my mind flaked away, and a cool wind swept through the black, taking my fragments with it. I'd become the pieces. I didn't know what I was leaving behind in this place. My body and mind were always warring with each other for a grasp of reality. Except even in this constant state of purgatory—in unreality—I still felt my essence, and my essence was separate and alone. And now... now instead of a union of mind, body and spirit, I was separated finally. The gurney had collapsed and what remained of me was draining away from the others and into the sewer. With my reflected, refracted image broken, filth was all that remained. I had become filth. The darkness blinked several times and a sudden golden burst lit it aflame. The cool wind carrying me turned to fire and scorched me as I collapsed onto solid ground. I shivered, the sudden chill assaulting my uncovered body.

"The park," Detherwheel whispered. I glanced at him and rolled my shoulders as he clung there excitedly.

I coughed and hugged myself. It was the park sure enough; the park where Sixela had found me fallen on the ground. Only, the park was drenched in a white blanket seldom seen in the city. Somehow, it had turned to winter. How long had I been gone? The trees were bare but for discolored rags of moss drooping sullenly from dead branches. Tired, I sat down in the snow and ran my hands over my face.

"Caw! Caw! We are cawed Murder. Get it! Caw! Caw!"

I looked up and shook my head. A black cloud of crows hovered in front of me. They stuck together in the form of a giant crow's head. I rubbed my eyes, not desiring to dialogue any longer. I wanted my abyss back.

"What about now?" Murder croaked. The cloud of black fluttered into the shape of a man. The man tipped his top hat and danced a jig. "Hmmm?"

"Great," I muttered.

"Fair enough. Next!" Murder said, floating above us in a billowing cloud of black and hovering there as if threatening to storm at any moment.

A man popped up from a nearby snowbank and jogged over to me. The man had no facial features. Instead, he had a gold prosthetic nose in the center of his blank, gray face. The only other things on his head were two saber length ears of solid gold that jutted from the side of his head like deadly horns. The man held his arms wide as if to embrace me. I scowled. Smoothing his golden robes, he pulled out a pretzel. I rolled my eyes. The pretzel was no pretzel, but a brain forced into the shape of one. He held his arm out, offering the pulsing, veiny thing to me. I gagged. Apparently offended, the man yanked up his shimmering robes, turned around and ran back to his snow heap to bury himself completely.

"What theatre!" I shouted emptily.

The cold was worsening. My senses were dull and the biting of the frost had grown sharp enough as to turn warm. I knew I didn't have long. A piece of black fluttered down from the cloud above. A lone crow perched on a thin branch of the closest tree and blinked at me. In its beak it held an ornate, silver key in the shape of a scythe.

"The key to living is to know that you're dying, and that dying is the key to living. Unlock life and death by being thankful for them both. Do you here that knocking? It's only the cries of all that have come before, and all that will come after. They say, 'We do not remember!'" The crow drowsily swung the scythe key back and forth as if trying to hypnotize me. "What is your why? Without a why, no how can be endured." The crow's voice was shrill and ancient, as withered as the branch it stood on.

The crow flew back up to Murder, and the cloud descended in front of me, this time in the shape of a skeleton. It stretched out a feathered hand and placed the scythe key against my neck. I pressed my neck welcomingly against the silver blade.

"The maze is unlocked," Murder said.

I was too numb to feel the cut. The warmth of my spilling blood comforted me as I returned to black. As soon as the black came, light interrupted. Stone walls spread out beneath me. I hovered above what appeared to be an infinite bleak and gray maze.

"See there in the distance?" Detherwheel said.

I shrugged. I'd forgotten the lizard was on my shoulder like usual and he hung there tightly, afraid of what surely would be a fatal fall.

"Open your eyes! There's a shadow and there's a light. We must escape them both. I don't know which one is trustworthy, but I know that each of them is coming for you."

I put my hand over my eyes to block out the harsh glare of the dreary fog that surrounded me. It pulsed like a heartbeat, electric blue throbbing in the mist. The fog parted where Detherwheel ostensibly pointed, making it hard to tell exactly where with his little legs clinging to me and his head sticking out like a dart. I looked at his beady eyes and back to the parting mist.

A figure cloaked in a cloud of black hunched forward, gangly and malformed like a rotting reaper. The cloud clung to the figure's form like a shadow, moving and hissing. Hissing! I could hear the cloud as if it were a part of me! The shadow's head looked up at me.

"How can I be hearing that monster!" I shouted. The hissing sounded so loud, I wasn't sure if it were from within my own mind, outside it or both.

"Look there!" Detherwheel said.

His tail stuck out like a staff and I whirled around in the opposite direction, very aware of my hovering form suddenly feeling very heavy. I gulped and peeked over my shoulder at the shadow I'd turned from but it was gone, enveloped in the pulsing mist. A subtle, low pitched groaning rumbled in the backdrop as if the fog were yawning. A putrid scent tore through the air and I dropped to the ground as the stench of rot filled my senses.

A glowing orb of light was there to greet me. I stared into it, squinting my eyes in an attempt to discern if a figure was hidden inside. I thought I saw blinking eyes, but the brilliant white-yellow light was overpowering. It increased in its splendor, and I stumbled backwards.

"Run, you fool!" Detherwheel said, thumping my head with his tail.

I sprinted away, not looking back. I ran and ran, turning as abruptly and randomly as possible. After several minutes of such a frenetic pace, I slowed to a walk and sat in a corner with my head against the cold wall. I listened but couldn't hear anything other than random yawning and humming from the mist above. The smell of decay was gone, or at least hindered by the distance. As a matter of fact, the only sense I felt was the coolness of the stone wall. The air seemed nonexistent and everything was absolutely still and silent but for the moaning mist.

A subtle clacking echoed nearby. It was followed by the rustling drag of what sounded like a robe.

"The shadow?" I asked.

"No," Detherwheel said, frowning as he looked towards the nearing sound. "A different kind."

I didn't budge. I was still exhausted from my desperate flight, and still numb from the frigid cold of the park. I wished I had a cloak of shadows, at least then I'd feel more secure. There was no hiding here. I waited, too tired to fear.

A small figure rounded the corner. With a blank face, I watched her approach. She was a small child with long black hair pouring out from her raised hood. She was garbed in a black, ragged cloak with holes and tears all over it. Her face was bone-white. I looked closer. No, her face was bone. She was a skeleton.

She clutched a rusty scythe in her right hand. A death's-head hawkmoth was perched on top of the curved blade, lazily stretching its wings. The moth was missing the signature death's head mark on its body, but it had an actual skull for a head with two curved, ram-like horns sprouting from its forehead. A red jewel glowed in the center of its skull. The moth was almost as large as the blade it was perched on. I didn't know which of these characters to fear more. I yawned. I had almost forgotten that I was still too tired to be afraid.

The moth spoke first, its voice crisp like the rustling of leaves. "Will you be crushed by your iniquities?"

"My only iniquity is giving you my time." I smiled and leaned back against the wall with both hands behind my head.

"Your time?" the child said. Her voice was demonically deep and innocently high at the same time, as if two different voices spoke together. "Look at Skully's gemstone." She pointed at the moth's head with a long, double-jointed bone finger. "That stone was bought with time. It was created from the depths of being. Its price is an eternal scar of decay. I am as I am because of this. Skully can no longer soar like the hawk she once was. Now she is a symbol of death. I have become more than the symbol." Her words were ancient and aching, each syllable sounding as if it rode a shrill wind echoing in a cavernous grave.

"A stupid bargain. The gem is shiny though." I grinned and laughed so violently that I threw my head back and banged it against the wall. I yelped and rubbed at it. "Stupid," I muttered.

"Your time is not yours. All time is ours."

"Because we all die? How profound!" I rolled my eyes and resumed my previous posture of relaxation.

"The stone is the price of life. The stone is death. To wear its mark is to be called hideous. To wear its mark is to be called death. Yet, to wear its mark is *to be* life."

"Sounds expensive." I yawned. Detherwheel lounged in the hollow between my neck and shoulder as if on a hammock, apparently bored.

"Shall we skewer this unworthy wretch, Mistress?" Skully said, aiming her horns and thrusting them at me in preparation.

"No. He must see through the symbol."

I shook my head. "What if I refuse? Please, end me! I'm so sick of this game. The quest was always designed to fail, made to be incomplete. A perfect end you two could bring… you delicious duo of delightful death!" I laughed at my alliteration. "Delicious! Why, you're just a child! You do not know death!" I jumped to my feet in a burst of anger. Detherwheel scrambled onto his usual shoulder-perch and clung there.

"And you?" she said.

"I don't know!" I threw my hands down in disgust, helpless in the face of such absurdity. "Helpless," I mumbled.

I smiled and walked closer to the child's scythe. I pressed my face against Skully's horns.

"Now, Mistress?" Skully begged.

"I'm a child!" cried the girl. Her bone's wavered, and skin and sinew sprouted. She grinned happily.

She was angelic. Precious. Beautiful. To think she had worn the mask of death so dreadfully. To know such beauty and light were locked beneath made me want to weep!

Clandestine life revealed, the now precious child pristine with being, tore off her cloak. Her body was shrouded in shadow. The same shadow belonging to the monster. The shadow enveloped her, blotting out her glory. I cried out and reached for her. The scythe dropped, narrowly missing my shoulder. I heard a squeak but thought nothing of it as I watched the dear child be taken away in the darkness.

The cloud covered her entire body, the only evidence of life in the blackness was a glowing red light. At least she had her Skully. A pointless thought. I dropped to my knees and watched as the glow intensified. The black gloom burst into a red glow. I shielded my face. As the light relaxed, I chanced a glance and laughed. A bundle of red balloons bunched together like a giant tower floated upwards. The girl's laughter poured down onto me from somewhere in the center of all those rising balloons. She no longer spoke with two voices but with one. Her mirth was childlike and pure. I couldn't see her but I knew she was somewhere in the midst of that mountain of balloons, ascending higher and higher.

The shadow monster had been innocent after all. The child was free! Free! I laughed, spinning in circles as I watched the balloons ascend into the mist. I stared for some time at the spot where they'd been enveloped in. I could have sworn I saw a hand wave, and a blinking red glow through the fog. But now, I was alone once again in the nothingness of this senseless maze. The mist was silent now.

"Just a child! A child! No monster after all." I shook my head and turned to my shoulder. Detherwheel wasn't there. I swallowed, turning behind me. The scythe hadn't missed.

Detherwheel was headless on the ground, his dead eyes accusatory and afraid, encased in an endless rage never to be satisfied. I sighed and sat down beside his body. Why couldn't it have been his tail? At least that could grow back! Yet, I wasn't sad at his death. I couldn't even mourn the loss of the only creature in this nightmare that had remained by my side through most everything. If anything, I felt free. His judging gaze was forever shut. He couldn't tell Sixela of my failures now. I scooted back over to my corner, ignoring the scraping stone against my skin. Sixela. Always Sixela. Was I far enough in her quest now? I leaned back on the wall and waited. The monster of light was due.

"Come! I am alone!" I cried, a bit startled at the exuberance marking my voice. I rubbed at my throat and waited.

"You're never alone." Like a Byzantine chant, the words spoken carried themselves in a haunting, beautiful, and sober way that inexplicably terrified me.

The light appeared in front of me, an intense glow overwhelming all of my senses. Warmth. I was warmth. I smiled, then started laughing at the sudden waves of ecstasy.

"What are you?" I asked. "What kind of monster are you?"

"I'm no monster. I'm here to help you fulfill your desires. To help you complete your quest."

"Much nicer than the other monster," I said with a squint.

I crossed my arms as I stood up. With a start, I looked down at myself as I felt the cool brush of cloth against my skin. I was wearing a robe split vertically down the middle with black on the left and crimson on the right.

"Clothed in deeds of your righteousness. Your righteousness is yours. Yours," the light said, hovering there in a large orb that seemed to steadily increase in brilliance and power as we spoke.

"Is it righteous if I told you that I hate my neighbor as I see fit?" I chuckled, embracing the role of the mad fool. It was the only part that I felt fit to play.

"It is your decision on who your neighbor must be, and how that neighbor relates to you. You can only hate what you know. You can only love what you do not." Its voice was still that ancient chant, a choir of baritone voices rumbling like angelic thunder.

"My decision is to kill you. Is that righteous?" I tilted my head and raised an eyebrow, failing to hold back a mocking smile.

"By your hand, your deeds are as righteous as any other."

"You're serious, aren't you? A relativist then? What makes a deed righteous, might I ask?"

"If you act according to your will, and not to the judging gaze of others. To be righteous, you need to act as yourself. You need to be absolutely free—then whatever you do is righteous."

"I feel like I've been here before," I said, massaging my cheekbones.

This was the same freedom dialogue I'd already had too many times on this stupid quest. I leaned against the wall and pulled my robe tighter to my chest. I rubbed my temples and ran my fingers through my hair. I knew how to deal with this line of thought; Graveyard had been helpful enough there. Yet I couldn't quite place my finger on it, but there was an odd uneasiness here. Like a ripple of reality bled through this terror. And that reality— this being's presence was intoxicating. I giggled as its light seemed to deepen as if aware of my thoughts. Clearing my throat, I attempted to focus.

"You can't be free without being your true self, I agree. But to be your true self you need to live for the infinite. Can you be free when everything is finite? If everything is ending, are we free when dying is our only absolute choice?" I said.

"You speak as if death destroys meaning. I ask you this then: if your infinity existed, how can the finite find meaning in what is unknowable, in what is beyond the perishing?" The light blinked, its glow decreasing for the moment.

"I say that you cannot have meaning without perfection to pursue. True perfection must be inexhaustible, so meaning must be a struggle to always keep pursuing perfection. If perfection can be achieved, the moment of achievement renders everything meaningless once more. So, the infinite is necessary for one who is finite to truly live with any truth, with any purpose, with any meaning, and with any hope."

"To pursue what is never ending is just as meaningless as something that ends forever. Either way, the goal is always beyond. The struggle against death is a meaning in itself."

The light's voice had lost its heavenliness and taken on a darker tone that I could only think of as satanic. The angels of this choir had apparently been replaced by demons. Though, these demons were making some valid points.

Validity aside, I was tired of philosophizing. I was tired of these dialogues. Yet, I never could resist trying to prove my point, even if I agreed with what the other person was saying, but now… now I wanted to collapse. I closed my eyes and tore off the robe, turning my back to the light and sitting down. The mist hummed rhythmically and the light howled. I smashed my head against the wall to make it stop. It didn't stop, the noise only intensified and my head hurt. Something gently brushed my shoulder.

The light was gone and everything was silent as I stared in awe. Sixela stood there in a flowing gown of black. She brushed my hair out of my eyes.

"Poor boy," she cooed, rubbing the bump on my head.

"I just want this to stop," I whispered. "I just want to rest."

"Rest is not for one such as yourself. But I have something better." She smiled and reached into the folds of her skirt. She handed me a gleaming sliver pistol with swirls of flame etched into its sides. "Kill me. Kill yourself. Do both. Do one. Either way you will not rest. But you can do."

I started to shake my head but she grabbed my neck and held me still. She placed the gun in my hand and I immediately pointed it at my head. Then my arm shook and I found myself pointing the gun right at Sixela's chest. Her irises were like flashing supernovas and her pout a black hole—I was being consumed by her splendor. I had to end it. I had to. Did she want me to shoot her? Would this prove that I wanted nearness, and would destroy our distance?

About to squeeze the trigger, I heard the faint echoes of joy. Laughter. A breeze tickled my neck and I heard the chuckles of children. Like the banquet before, the children's bliss was here to save me. My body shook and everything whirled. I fell on my face and clutched at the ground, trying to steady myself. The innocent laughter sounded louder this time, as if they were around the corner. I wept at their joy. I wept at my lack.

"I want rest," I cried. "I want rest!"

A pulling and then a prodding. And I was gone from the maze. Sixela was nowhere to be found. Birds fluttered, singing indifferent songs of selfishness. The air was fresh and alive with ripples of breezes that curled the lengthy grass and wrapped me in a ripe and fruity perfume. I was back by the foothills. I looked up and my city was above. The skull-moon had vanished. Was I ready to finish my quest? Was I really going to be allowed to finally rest?

No. I knew better than that. A rumble shook beneath me. I sat on the ground, exhausted. Soil crumbled and collapsed into a giant hole that was several feet in front of me, and from the depths a bright green dragon emerged. As giant as it was, larger than any of the foothills, it wasn't exactly menacing. It had no teeth. It had no horns. Its eyes blinked and looked around, apparently bored.

"Sir?" I said.

"Die a lizard, come back a lizard."

"Detherwheel?" I said, recognizing his squeaky voice which was ill-suited for his current frame.

I didn't know whether to be happy or sad, as his return must've meant that my quest was going to inevitably continue.

"Yes. Yes. But why do you sit? Do you not see the wells that remain?"

I sighed, standing to look around me. Sure enough, the wells were still there. I hadn't even noticed them, so hopeful for an end as I was. The well we had entered to get to the skull-moon was crumbled in a heap of stone. The other wells gleamed pristine and impatient. I refused to keep going. If one well took that long, and went to so many places... I wasn't prepared for another five.

"No."

"No?" he said.

"I cannot go through that again... and then again, and again. I'm done."

I started to sit back down but Detherwheel lowered his head and picked me up by the robe that I'd previously torn off. Now it was miraculously whole on my body once more as if to serve this one purpose.

"Look around!" he roared, his breath sulfurous as it washed over my body.

From this vantage point I could see for miles, and I almost blacked out from the horror. Behind the six wells on top of each hill, there were twelve more hills each with a well; behind the twelve were 24, behind the 24 were 48, and so on and so on, always increasing twofold—an infinite expanse of wells circling outwards.

"You can't..." I whispered.

"Every well. Every last one of the infinitude must be finished."

"Put me down," I growled.

Detherwheel huffed but relented, bowing his head and letting me drop from far enough up that it hurt when I crashed to the ground.

"You think all these wells will tempt me? Is this how she wants me to live? To pursue her?" I chuckled, wiping the grass from my knees and smoothing the robe back down over them. "I'll live forever! Forever exploring the depthless depths of the wells. Learning, loving, longing! The immortality! The meaning at last!" I threw my hands up and cackled with my head reared back and my eyes wildly searching the sky in between. "Just because it is endless, does not mean that I don't want an end. The endless end I want is one that is always expanding, yet always completely fulfilling. That is a meaningful meaninglessness! That is finite infinity!" I smiled and closed my eyes, nodding to myself. "My paradox is greater, because without paradox there is no reason not to lie down and stop." I paused, wiping my eyes that were soaked from my crazed laughter. I gravely turned to Detherwheel and peered up at him with sympathy. "Without paradox I might as well keep moving. Regardless, everything is a deception." I breathed heavily and sat down, resting my head on my fist, lost in emptied thoughts and impatient for something or someone to come.

"Failure."

Her voice shook me. I shivered. I stood and faced her. She rode atop Detherwheel's head. Oddly, even as close as she was now, she had never felt so far. This was demonic distance. Delusion. The result of my decadent detachment with reality. My fantasy a consuming illusion that was truly a nothing, emptier than all the wells this world had. Against my being. Against reality.

"You never even knew me," she laughed.

I looked at her one last time, appreciating her glory. A scarlet dress pooled around her like blood. Her eyes burned with blue fire. I turned and ran. I ran and ran, till the hills, the wells, the everything, blurred by. I ran faster than Hermes. I ran faster than flight. I refused to look back but the nape of my neck was always hot as if flame were mere inches away. I ran and ran some more. The heat never let up. The blurring wells and hills slowed as I realized I was coming to a precipice. Apparently, this infinity had an end after all.

There was no more room for running. I stopped in desperation, the fire still burning behind. Sixela sung beautifully in a melodious roar. I had reached the precipice and the only way forward was over the cliff and into the abyss. Perhaps the dragon was better than the abyss, for at least I knew it.

Then Bog spoke, "Leap, for this moment is forever."

I looked up to see a flaming yellow sun, warm and powerful. Bog spun rays of sunlight from the middle of it. I gasped and my chest felt as though it weighed a ton. The fire behind me intensified its heat. I looked down at the center of my chest and saw a red hole swirling like a bloody whirlpool. Not understanding how I knew what to do, I did it anyway. I thrust my hand inside and pulled out a smooth stone in the shape of an apple that was twice the size of my hand. It reeked of rot. Tiny beasts with large animal heads crawled across like ants. I wanted to drop it but was afraid. I had to fill this hole with something. I had to fill it with a leap. The fire burned behind me and Sixela's song went silent. I looked back one last time to gaze at her beauty but she wasn't there. Nothing was there. I was alone on a precipice, and everything around me was an abyss. The sky went black and I tripped and fell off the cliff.

As the distance of my fall increased, the cliff disappeared and it became so dark that it seemed bright. I smiled as the warmth of reality wrapped its loving truth around my neck. My breath grew thin. As the blackening light enveloped me, a terrible thought overtook me.

If I stumbled into the abyss, was it not a leap but a fall?

Chapter 7

Sunday

A long fall into a deeper forever had brought me here. For long I have toiled. I am alone with myself, but not alone by myself. Bog's warm orb spins out its endless strands of sunlight, never ceasing its tangle in the white sky, but still remaining high above. He never spoke to me anymore, at least not how he once did long ago. Yet I felt I knew him better than ever. I could feel his warmth.

The land around was arid and scorched red. Sharp-squared walls of rusty-hued stone surrounded me, and I stood there at home in the bottom of the canyon where a small river that was a muddy gold bent around my stone hut. I'd settled here for the simple reason that to wander was no longer necessary. I had what I needed and did not need to stray. It was not instant and took much struggle, but I'd submitted to the sunlight and strengthened my everything. Not just mind or will, not mere imagination, but I'd dug into the soil and became a part of the earth I'd for so long fled.

No longer a prisoner in my mind, I broke free by building my body along with this hut, and in doing so, I at last felt home existing fully as myself—mind, body, and soul. I trained hard in this manner so as to know the dust I'd sprung from, and in doing so, better know my redeemed skeleton. I bent down and held the warm dirt in my hand and let it run through my stained fingers. I breathed in deep and smiled up at the sun.

What had that quest even been about, but for my own diversion from my tired lot in life? How long had I sat here at this very river and stared into the muddy waters, wondering what the purpose of any of it had been? And then wondering if my leap had been a hop, for hops can go back and forth while a leap is meant to be forever. I'd wrestled much with the silence of this land. But this silence was not the kind that made you scream, this was the kind that while uncomfortable at first, gradually filled every crevice of your soul until you became like the very rocks of the canyons— solid and still.

There was no black speck in the sun, but Bog was in my chest. I knew this, for how could I forget that my chosen fall into him—the moment—was my new heart? The silence did not bother me. No, it made me stronger. I smiled, here I stood with not a stitch on my back, stronger than ever… and yet… the lingering whisper of unfinished promises bit at me like insects. No matter how hard I worked, the biting of my conscience only seemed to worsen. I knew something was going to change, and soon. She was still out there on her dragon. She still clung to the corner of my mind like a nightmarish shadow. I could not forget. Cursed be the lingering of my mind's eye!

"Hello, hermit!" a voice called.

I turned from the soil to see a sorry sight. A hunched husk of a man limped towards me. His face was covered with dirty bits of stubble sprouting like patches of weeds. His hair was white and greasy, hanging in long uneven strands from beneath a stained black ballcap. He smiled a brown-toothed grin, his eyes downcast now that he was face to face with me. I clenched my fists at the intrusion, and warily eyed him up and down, looking behind and waiting for some trap. Years with nobody, and now at last a somebody had come, and he was a wretch!

"I am no hermit," I muttered.

"You dress the part," he said with a laugh, looking at my unclothed flesh and spitting into the dirt.

He mumbled to himself as I scowled, and he hung his head in a show of deference. I could not tell if it was an act or not. He peeked up at me as I continued staring.

"A beggar coming to my canyon of silence... Why now? Who has sent you?"

"My own despair. All I beg for is a reason."

"A reason for what?" I crossed my arms and flexed them menacingly as I stared down at him.

"You in your strength and courage have survived much. Your silence is one that destroys most. You need no diversion. So, I ask for a reason."

I frowned. "Speak clearly."

"A reason why you continue so. You are stronger. You are better. But why?"

I took a long breath and turned away, not for lack of answer, but from a flash of familiarity. How many of these fruitless dialogues had I had during that pointless quest? Was this a sign that the old world I'd thought I'd leapt from was returning? I feared my lingering thoughts of her, and my subtle doubts of myself, were bringing back the shadows of the sunless sky.

"I have two songs to sing to you. I sing them for a reason. Perhaps you could give it to me after."

I stared over the beggar, looking for the past he inevitably was bringing in. He hummed and clapped his hands, and then started to sing in a rasping voice.

Beggars beg. Sinners sin. Beggars lie. Sinners win.

His back straightened and he stood tall, eye to eye with me. He smiled, his eyes suddenly clear and sure.

Eyes like fallen snow in a summer sun.
Maelstrom irises burn through cloudless sky.
Antarctic current, both wind and sea:
Iceberg pulls, I crash into only me

He pointed at me and nodded, finishing his song with a snap.

"Me? Do you speak of yourself or me?" I said. I knew whose eyes he spoke of. I shuddered.

"You don't see her in me? You don't see her in you? Well then of course you can't see you in me!"

I grabbed him by the shoulders and shook him. "Where is she?" I screamed.

He laughed and so I shook him harder. My body of earth was not enough to make this demon of dark speak true. I threw him to the ground and stepped over his useless form.

"Where are you?" I shouted far off into the canyons. The ancient red stone answered me with a hoarse echo. "Sixela!" I yelled.

My chest ached at using her name. I hadn't even allowed myself to think it since my leap, yet now I shouted it. The canyon did not respond with an echo as I yelled her name again. I turned at the sound of laughter from the broken beggar. I kicked his decrepit body and he laughed louder.

"You still have not given a reason," he said through bloody lips, spitting up red into the dust like spilled paint.

I took a deep breath and looked down at him. "You want my reason? My why? What if I answer your question with the same: why not? I build because the moment I don't, I crumble. This is no quest, it is living. To live is to do more than simply be, more than simply maintain. I'm a house that stands by not merely being built on rock, but by continually being built up by the rock it stands on. And this rock is infinite." I spread my arms wide and breathed deeper. I would not let this fool tear it all down.

The beggar struggled to his feet and I let him stand. He was back to being hunched over again, like a beggar should be.

"Spoken like a hermit. Is this house only filled with you? Are its halls empty? You fill your rooms with striving, with goals? That is not a reason. Perhaps I was wrong. Perhaps you do live in diversion, for it, even."

I frowned. I thought back to Graveyard. I thought back to my conversation in the maze with the terrible light. A lifetime ago. So long. What was it... what had been my answer then? Or theirs?

The light had said it did not matter. I was my own reason in my freedom. I remembered my response. Pursuit of an endless perfection. I suppose that was what I had been doing while working here. And my body had responded. I was built like the gods. My mind had reached heights unimagined as passion was not my master but a willing partner that worked in tune with my very being. I was whole... yet, was I? Where was my reason? A pursuit of eternal perfection, an unreachable goal that was always being reached. A cup always full while still increasing in its size and fullness. Was that what I had here? Or were my rooms empty?

"I see you think. I respect your silence. I once more see your fullness. I only ask that you make sure your fullness is not the empty air of diversion." He stood straight again and placed his dirty hands on my shoulders. "You called out Sixela's name. You still linger even after your leap. This is natural. It is not meant to be forgotten, not meant to be ignored. It is meant to be used. To transcend."

"I... I see. I thought my foundation needed strengthening. My infinite foundation. How foolish. How long can one stay at the bottom of the canyon? We are not only earth."

I crouched and picked up a handful of dust again. I looked at it closer and could see myself in each speck. But when fashioned together, when all the specks gathered into an ocean, what then was I to do? All my selves as one infinite whole, power and promise, waiting to surge. How many forgot that they were both like the single speck and the entire desert too? It was a matter of sight and focus. Where was the will directed? I had the goal of always building. Yet my building was spreading out and not filling in and rising above. And so, I had no reason.

I nodded and let the dust drop from my hands as I stood. "I have none. My reason is I am searching for the reason. In the heat of this sun, you cannot evaporate. There are no mirages. The desert is not one of dust." I paused as I looked at the veins pushing against my skin. An image of clear water flowed in my mind. "There is living water surging through my very veins. Not begging to be spilled, not begging to recreate, but begging to be as it is meant to be. Blood burned red by the sun, pulling the being higher and higher, right into its always forever core. This blood is meant to be shared. It is blood purchased by infinity." I smiled at the beggar, and he smiled back.

"We both beg. I begged for your reason, but you beg for what was already bought. We are one in our struggle towards sublimity."

I looked up at the eternal sun and imagined I could see the child and her balloons. She had said that death must be worn. Naked under the sun, I looked up at it and nodded. My death was my blood and so was my life.

"Why did you sing her song?"

He sighed. "Her wintertide comes to bury this summer in a cold white sea, but only if you do not burn through its depths."

I frowned. "You said she was in you and me. I do not want her. I want nothing to do with her." I looked at the beggar who now looked away, though he stood straight; his averted glance was fitting of his title.

He mumbled, with his head down yet shoulders squared. "In my soon coming end I can see that there is something new *above* the sun that the grave brings and it's terrifying." He looked up into my eyes. "Can you die without ever flying over and through the abyss your spider led you to? Was it a web? A cocoon? Or was it a silk thread dangling from an eternal sun? As the clock sings its lonely decay, I see the end of the rope fraying and I can only see eternity. I can only see your one strand as an essential nothingness in the shadow of forever. What do you do? What do *you* do? She is coming. You mustn't do nothing."

He took a deep breath and hummed, repeating his rhyme: *Beggars beg. Sinners sin. Beggars lie. Sinners win.*

He looked up at the sun and said, "To believe is to beg. To sin is to live. Forgive us, for we have lived and not begged. To beg is to deceive. Truth needs no beggars, for truth cannot be swindled. Then we must be swindlers, not beggars. We sell our lonely wares. The lovely death knell of our action. *Our* action. The silk is fraying. What kind of silk is it?" He stopped his questioning the sky and turned to me. "Does the spider love?" he asked.

I shook my head at the question, foregoing an answer as I already knew. In the far distance behind us a shriek suddenly sounded. A piercing wail, high pitched and full of death. The lone shriek filled the canyon with its singular voice, and behind it came another sound. I knew it. A roar. A dragon's roar. Icy fire surged through the canyon walls, and a green dragon emerged from the blue flames. It screamed. Its mouth was filled with dripping fangs, teeth crowding the cavernous maw like stalagmites. And there on the beast's back, a woman in white rode. I swallowed. My chest contracted and my heart rattled inside me. I tried to breathe, tried to believe that I was not hers, but it was for naught. She truly was too great for me, even as I stood now.

"Let me sing for you!" The beggar cried, looking at me and not Sixela. "No, not for... but *as* you." He clasped both my hands. I turned away from the dragon.

I fear I am caught.

I fear I am naught.

Does the spider care?

I fear I am free.

I fear I am me.

Does the spider stare?

Bog the spider always sees.

Bog the spider is in me.

Can a stumble become a leap?

Can a fall become a rise?

Bog the spider is forever free.

Bog the spider weaves eternity.

Bog loves.

"Bog!" I called.

"Bog!" Sixela shrieked as her dragon swooped down behind me, crashing into the red dirt and spraying up clouds of dust.

I knew he loved. I knew that in his silence in this valley, that he loved. I looked at the constant sun and smiled. Did I want him to return as a tiny speck in my ear? Or did I want him to remain as lofty as he'd been when crawling across the sun and saving me from that awful quest? But the beggar's song... in me. Could he be both? Was my house empty? My heart beat. Its still pumping blood was one of mercy and gratitude. I lived. I smiled and turned to Sixela.

"Why now?" I asked.

She patted her dragon's head and he lowered her to the ground. She wore a white robe that bared her chest, the one I still remembered when she, or the phantasm of her, had stomped Bog in my bile.

"Detherwheel and I felt you were ready. Strong," she said, looking down at my exposed body and smiling.

I scoffed. "Your perfect beauty never left my mind. I would be a fool to forget such perfection. But in this peace here, where I built myself as me, you are just another stone."

Her elegant eyebrows, sharp like scythes, stormed over her electric eyes as she glared into mine.

"And your beggar?" Detherwheel said. His old squeak was gone. He roared now—a voice of thunder paired frighteningly with Sixela's lightning glare.

"He's not mine." I turned to look at him.

"No, but we are yours," he said. "I have found the reason I was looking for. He says that his reason is infinity."

"So you hide in non-existent future?" Detherwheel said with puffs of smoke trickling out from his nostrils as he chuckled in a strange and rumbling wheeze.

"My reason is the infinity of now. It's the moment." I breathed in deep, my eyes looking up at the sun again.

"Do you not see me here?" Sixela screamed. She leapt from Detherwheel's back and onto the ground, her breasts bouncing and her robe sliding lower.

I gulped and grit my teeth as not to be overcome with lust. And I'd thought it had fled! But no... her stone was still a part of my building. I had to acknowledge it and watch how it weathered. There was no removing it without toppling an essential part of me. But it was a stone that needed polishing. It was a stone that needed restoration.

"Your beauty is a sublimity in and of itself. Sixela, how can I see others without seeing you?" I stepped closer to her and she stretched out her slender hand. "The beauty of obsession. The transcendence of sight, distance devolved into an avenue of truncated adoration. I cut out my heart and used it as a looking glass. But none of this is you. It is my own doing. Myself. And in myself responding to yourself in such a way, your stone is mine, but only in me. I exist through not existing in you. This... you near me... cannot be. It cannot because it never was. Your stone in me, is my heart's architecture of your beauty. I need it. But you don't. So why are you here?"

Her hand stopped short of my face. She tremored, her face twitching and eyes squinting at me. It was a face of doubt, of deceit. She looked at me, pulled back her hand, and nodded.

"My beauty will be a part of your pinnacle. That is right. But I must go. That was what this quest was for. Your building up. Your seeing that my me, was really your you. We are as we are."

My chest tightened, and longing burned a hole inside. I wanted to grab her, to kiss her flower petal lips. To never taste her perfection, to only know my image of it... it was almost enough to burn me to ash. But I was a house built of stone, on a foundation of even harder stone. There was no burning it down.

"Then how does this quest end?" I said. "I'd thought it was over at my leap. Yet here you are." Tears gathered in my eyes. I knew an end with her was coming.

"This quest was never for me. It was for you. I am only great because you exalt me so." She stepped backwards and pressed her hand against Detherwheel's cheek.

"Beggar, what should I do?" I asked. "I am tired of silence."

He stepped closer to me. "If the reason is not her, nor was it ever, then you must act according to this reason that truly is. That of the moment. What is it, you row towards?" He smiled, and his skin fell away. A skeleton. And to dust he collapsed.

Sixela pressed her chest against Detherwheel and kissed his cheek. He purred like a satanic cat and belched fire into the heavens. She climbed onto his head and sat there aloft again.

Detherwheel looked at me with his beady, slit eyes and said, "All the wells you ignored, yet in the driest canyon you have found a well of infinite worth. Why is it that you ran?"

"Because I saw no point in playing your game any longer."

"Yet you continued here?" he said.

"Quest or not, I continued here because I fell in love with the joys of building through daily existence. No fools bothering me with frivolous dialogues on the meaning of meaning, or the meaninglessness of it all. No, here I was left alone with myself, and I could either build or decay. I chose the former."

"So your own well never went dry. But we came for a reason. Not your beggar's reason either," he said.

"And what reason is this?" I said, looking directly at Sixela.

"You still wanted me." She smiled, tracing her finger down the center of her chest. "Even in your... development," she eyed me up and down again, "you still had not finished your quest. Do you remember what your quest was for?"

I thought back to what seemed to be many lifetimes ago. "A quest to go home." I shook my head. "Home. That was never my apartment. I'm a fool." I shook my head harder and laughed.

"To go home you must kill me," Sixela said.

"Never!" I shouted. "I will not play games."

"I am not dead, for I never lived. Remember that I am your stone. There must be restoration."

"You must go home, and you must build it better," Detherwheel said. His cold eyes closed, and he breathed in a loud rush of ashen air.

"So consume your vision of me. This image you see, must be yours alone," she said.

She glared down at me now with the eyes of a goddess, and she reached her hand up towards the sky, and a red bolt of lightning struck her fingertips, leaving a sword of pearl-pink energy in her hand. Detherwheel belched a pillar of fire into the sky. I stood there as firmly as one could, unclothed and unarmed as I was. But out of the corner of my eye, I saw that where the beggar had perished, a silver scythe rested in his place. I reached down and held it before me. A swirl of wind gathered in the canyon, whipping up dust about the three of us. My hair flew around me like tatters, and I clutched my scythe harder and stared up at her.

"Sixela the Great! You are not too great. You are another stone!" I yelled, the wind whipping my words about as if adding to their force.

She grimaced, then smiled at my words. She shrieked as Detherwheel pounced at my body. I rolled out of the way, wielding the scythe like a farmer ready to gather the best of crops. My tares to reap first! The wheat would grow taller for it! I swept the blade at Detherwheel's trunky legs, but the blade cut only air as he leapt skyward and flapped his scaly, purple wings.

Sixela pointed her blade of light down at me, and pink lightning shot from its tip. I held up the scythe in desperation and stood my ground, the silver blade somehow stopping the tear of light in its tracks as it fizzled out like a dying flame.

She yelled, her fiery voice despite it all, making my heart flutter with longing. She was right. I had to stop this. How was it I still longed for her even as I fought to tear her away from my heart? With her lusty yell, another pink branch of light cracked at me just as red-blue flame burned down with Detherwheel's roar.

I thrust the scythe once more in front of me, letting the pummel of energy meet my blade. Only, this time I refused to let it dissipate unused; my tares to tear through! I yanked back the scythe and spun in a circle, flinging back the ball of now crackling pink-blue flame right at Sixela's beautiful head. I watched in horror as she was struck dead-on by my returned missile, and she fell from Detherwheel's hovering body and dropped through the air. I couldn't stop myself from running towards her falling form— an angel from heaven—I dove and caught her in my naked arms.

Her hair was like black silk spread across my arms, so long it brushed the ground though I held her high, cradling her like a child. She tiredly looked at me, and as if awakening, suddenly her eyes lit with blue fire and she scratched her way out of my arms, pushing me back and yelling. She stumbled backwards as Detherwheel roared and thrust his head between us. I grunted as my heart thudded, not from exhaustion but for desire. I wanted to stroke that creamy skin, breathe in that olive scent longer. I wanted to gaze at her marble flesh, those living sculpture features. I wanted her beauty again, longer!

Detherwheel opened his mouth, his black tongue a torch as flames burst out from the furnace of his lungs. The fire leapt at me and I dove to the dirt, rolling out of the flames but not fast enough to prevent my back being burnt. I screamed as the skin blistered, and I rolled away again as more flames followed. I scurried on all fours to my scythe.

Scooping it up, I yelled and charged straight at Detherwheel's throat as he breathed in for another fiery onslaught. I leapt into his mouth, tearing the scythe through his gums in a circle as if harvesting wheat. Black blood spewed and his teeth fell free like broken icicles. His mouth remained propped open, perhaps out of shock, but he shrieked as I continued cutting, the sound so thunderous that my own blood dripped from my ears to join his black blood which already covered me.

The heat was unbearable, and I knew flames would come, so I reared back and flung the scythe down his throat, leaping out of his mouth just as a stream of fire surged from the black caverns of his belly. He cried out in a strangled whimper, and snapped his jaws, screaming as he stretched his wings and fled, flying away and leaving me sprawled on the ground, weaponless. I lay there on my back and watched the clear sky.

The sun shined as bright as ever, and the dragon's silhouette only seemed to make it brighter.

"Forgot me?" Sixela said, her voice close to me and labored.

She looked over my fallen body and sighed. Her blue eyes had faded into a dull colorless gray. I could see life was no longer lingering in those bright irises. I stood up, grimacing at the numb itching pain of my burnt back. I squeezed my blood-blackened fists

and looked at the goddess, now mortal and alone.

I said, "All this time I wanted you... all this time I longed

for something. I didn't let myself consider what that something

was—passion drove me through and through. I reveled in my

irrationality." I shook my head and hobbled closer to her, but she

held up her hand to keep me at bay. Her sword, smaller now,

flickered into her hand, mere steel and not light. "I wanted myself

to be something. And all I needed to do was to find my home. I

remember the banquet, that awful decay... but the story makes

sense now. My hiding place, my refuge away from all that tears

down, that is the self. The something. Me. I tried to use you to

bring this, Sixela. I tried to whore out your beauty for my own

selfish lust and obsession. I am sorry." I reached out my arms in

surrender. She stepped backwards.

She smiled, her teeth like white shells on a bright beach.

"Stare at my beauty and remember its power and feeling. Use this,

always." I stepped closer and she yelled at me with both her hands

out, "You mustn't come closer! No more lingering! No more

attachment! Look, and through seeing, feel. In the spirit!" She pointed at her breast. "Now I go. Forever I will fade into a distance that is no longer demonic, but instead, nearer than reality itself could ever bring, through transcendence. Transcend me, by remembering what I was in your mind's eye."

She held her arms out wide with her head back and face aimed at the sun. She closed her eyes and smiled. I stared and stared, and as a sudden sunbeam burned in a pillar of light, swallowing her whole, I watched her fluttering irises burn bright blue into my spirit one last time, watching me watch back forever. And Bog's sun swallowed her, and the light dissipated, and she was no more.

I reached back to feel my blisters, and nearly knocked off the figure standing there on my shoulder.

"All my teeth! Gone!" Detherwheel whined at me from his old place on my shoulder, while holding his tail as if I might take that next.

"I am home. There is no quest to guide me on, Detherwheel," I said, letting out a long and deep breath.

"I'm here because I'm as much a part of you as her. What will you do with me then, your fearsome dragon foe that you wounded but did not yet slay?" Detherwheel said, defiance flashing in those familiar, beady eyes.

I nodded. "You aren't my guide. But you are mine. Let us build."

"And what of the spider?"

I looked up at the sun and waited.

I love.

Made in the USA
San Bernardino, CA
14 July 2020